Hunger of the Heart

White Buffalo MCs Book 1

By

Trinity Blacio

Copyright © 2017 by Trinity Blacio
ISBN: 978-1-68361-169-1
Cover art by Tibbs Designs and Decadent Publishing

Published by
Decadent Publishing Company, LLC

Look for us online at:
www.decadentpublishing.com

~A Note from the Author~

Welcome to my world of Motorcycles and hot, Native American men. If you had only so many days before the world was going to change what would you do? What would you start saving to help you survive?

Contact me at: trinityblacio@outlook.com

Warriors of old used to ride their mighty horses out into the night, searching for the enemy, hunting for food, and enjoying the land the Great Mother let them borrow. Those times have changed, and greedy men have taken their land. Cities, roads fill their once quiet world.

Born on separate reservations, a group of young men with hearts of old souls, long dead warrior's souls, ride together again, but this time they don't ride horses. Today, it's all about the motorcycle. Helping the desperate, following the call of the ancient spirits. They call themselves The White Buffalo MC and it's their job to get their people ready for the dark day, which was told to them long ago.

Greed will not steal the woman of his heart. Running Wolf will save his crazy gypsy, Kizzy, even if it means reverting to scalping the white man.

Chapter One

"Each of us seeks something in life, but it is what we do with it when we find it that is what counts." Running Wolf, President, White Buffalo MC

William Teter loomed over her bruised and broken body, his greasy hair hanging in his face. "I told you I'd have you one way or another. You think I'd allow some breed to take what's mine? I'd rather you be dead first, but, before that, I will sample what you give so freely away." He ripped at her clothes. Pleasure lit his eyes at her struggles. She tried to fight him, but it only seemed to excite him as he tore open the front of her blouse.

"No!" Kizzy screamed herself awake, almost dropping the laptop in the process. Once more, she had fallen asleep while searching the Internet in her little reading nook. But this wasn't a nightmare, it was more. Kizzy could feel it in her gut, and her late momma always told her never to ignore her instincts.

Kizzy wouldn't ignore this dream. In addition to good advice, her mother had passed along a gift and sometimes sent signs even now. This dream, though, seemed so real that the evil was still present in her tiny house. She checked her home, not missing any hidden places he could hide, as if afraid he'd pop out from somewhere. Time to move on.

Her gaze lowered to her laptop screen where the man, Running Wolf, leaned against his motorcycle, his attention focused on something off in the distance. A beaded headband confined the long, dark hair falling to his shoulders. She was drawn to him but still chilled by the resemblance to the evil man in her dream.

Kizzy scribbled the phone number from the website on a scrap of paper and shut her laptop down. She tried to relax, taking a deep breath, her attention on the woods surrounding her tiny house. She curled up in her little window seat and drew in energy from outside. Sometimes, the ground and plants talked to her. In mid-May, the flowers, trees, and her garden were off to a wonderful beginning. She had planted twice what she usually did, knowing her friends, the small group of Shawnee, would need every bit she could grow. She had also planted wild lettuce, berries, and any other thing she could think of between her property line and their small piece of land because their pride made it hard for them to accept "handouts."

She toyed with the piece of paper in her hand, debating on calling. Her friends wanted to keep their whereabouts quiet, but their children were hungry and, if what she heard was true, they had a bigger problem at hand.

The thought of William Teter going near her new friends brought up a protective streak in her. He was the most disgusting pig she had ever met. The man would do anything to steal the land Lone Star had purchased for his people.

Her gaze moved to the picture on the wall of her mom pointing a stick at her, needing some kind of connection with her. She'd been yelling, "*I swear you are a fierce warrior, my Kizzy. It will take a strong man to capture you.*" Kizzy missed her parents. Their deaths still fresh in her heart, a tear slid down her cheek.

The phone next to her rang and startled her out of her thoughts. Dread filled her as she noticed the number on the screen, and Kizzy moaned. *William Teter*. If she didn't answer it, the dickwad would show up at her front door. If he wasn't already out there, waiting for her next move. She shivered at the memory of the time she had spotted him with a pair of binoculars aimed at her house as she arrived home from visiting Rose and Lone Star.

"Hello, William. What do you want?"

"I thought maybe you'd like to grab something to eat? I know you were digging in your garden all day and must be awful tired," William said.

"No, thank you. I'm taking a hot bath and going to read a book. I told you I'm not interested. You need to find someone else and quit telling everyone you are going to marry me. It's not going to happen."

"Aren't you taking this hard to get a bit far? I've given you plenty of time to come to your senses, but I just might have to take a stronger approach. I will talk to you soon, my dear. Take your hot bath while I decide what our next step should be." The line went dead.

That was it. Kizzy had to call in this group and hope they could help her friends because she didn't think there was much time for her here. William was crazy and getting worse.

It had taken her over three months to settle into her new home. She finally had a thriving bed of medicinal and culinary herbs growing, but unless they could stop William Teter and his goonies for good, she'd have to move.

She dialed the number and hoped the articles on the web about The White Buffalo MC wasn't some hoax because, right now, they offered the only light on the dark path she and her friends seemed to be on.

***

Running Wolf played the message on the answering machine again and leaned back in his desk chair. "Milan, Ohio, is our next run." A long way from their warehouse in upper Michigan. His instincts demanded they get on the road. "Did you pull up all the records we'll need?"

Sun Bull leaned back in his chair, watching him and smiling. His second-in-command could be counted on to act on a moment's notice. "Yeah, it's just as the woman said. This William Teter and a few of the bankers want their land. I've sent Penn and Raining Tom there ahead of us. Penn's paying all the back taxes for the properties. That should help ease some of the burden for now. He is also working on buying a few other pieces of land around theirs. Raining Tom is stationed in the woods outside her home." He stood and reached over the desk to hand Running Wolf a file. "I also have that background check on this Kizzy Lala who called. She's a lot like us, but this woman has had a rough life. Her parents were murdered two years ago. The authorities never solved the case. She has an older brother, but he's down in Florida with his family. Why she went from Mississippi to Ohio, I have no idea." He shrugged. "The pictures aren't the greatest, but she is a beauty."

He didn't know why, but the idea of Sun Bull thinking this woman was attractive didn't sit well with him at all. Running Wolf opened the folder and understood why his friend had said what he did. The woman was striking, and the deep pain in her eyes drew him in like nothing else ever had. Protectiveness rose swiftly inside

3

him. The thought of her out there, someone threatening this vulnerable beauty....

Sun Bull grinned like a fool. "So you have found her. It's as the medicine man told us. I'll get the others ready while you gather yourself, my friend. We'll get there in time and protect what the Great Mother has deemed yours. It's good to know we have our other halves out there. A lot of our men were giving up hope, but this will revive them. Do you want to wait till tomorrow or ride out tonight?"

"Tonight. We don't know how much time they have, and this Teter gives off a very dark shadow." Running Wolf faced his friend, Sun Bull. "I was one of those who had given up. Seems I owe the Great Mother an apology for not believing."

"No, she understands, more than anyone, especially in this time. We have been working so hard to help our people, sometimes we forget to take time for ourselves." Sun Bull moved to the door, grabbing his files and leather. "We'll be waiting for you."

She was his woman. There could be no other reason for him to feel the way he did. All the signs the old medicine man had mentioned were there: his heart was beating fast, and an amazing peace had settled over him. They would ride to Ohio right away. Yes, by late tonight, they would be camped around her home, making sure she was safe while he courted her and took care of the problem at hand—Teter, and the mayor of Milan.

The phone rang, and he answered it while stuffing papers into his bag. "We have problems. You need to get here quick. This crazy Teter is stalking the woman in question. I can see him now, he's pacing back and forth outside her home, but he's not the only visible threat. Seems this woman is desired by the mayor also," his scout said.

"Do not allow anyone to enter her abode. I don't care if you have to tie him up. We will be there in a few hours." Running Wolf hung up and started for the door, dialing his friend Tack Duggan who worked for the Ohio State Patrol.

"Running Wolf, to what do I owe the honor of your call?" The teasing started right away as usual.

"Funny. I don't know if you patrol up by Milan, but I'm headed that way now. There is trouble, and I was kind of hoping you could extend your services for a Kizzy Lala who is in need of protection."

"You never ask for favors. She must be important. Not to worry. I owe you. Hell, my whole family owes you. We'll keep her safe until

4

you get there. I suppose you already have a man at the location?"

"Yes, Raining Tom is there, and so is Penn. Raining Tom is in the woods outside her home but says a William Teter was hanging around in the yard. One of the reasons I'm calling. If Teter attacks...."

"On my way. Talk to you soon," Tack said.

Over thirty men waited for him on their bikes, the new horses for warriors in this time period. "We ride and know this, the threat has already begun, so we have no time to waste. Raining Tom and our friend Tack will be waiting for us. Remember, Kizzy must be protected. Let's ride." He swung his leg over his bike and revved the engine. "Hold on, Kizzy, love, we are coming." His words carried into the wind as he pulled out of the drive, heading toward the highway and his destiny.

Chapter Two

"My love for Kizzy is like witnessing the sun rise over the hill, a never-stopping joy, for the first time." Running Wolf, President, White Buffalo, MC

Kizzy snuggled deep into her blankets, trying to ignore the roar of engines. It sounded as if her home had moved next to the highway instead of the little clearing in the woods. What the hell was all that racket? It had to be...Running Wolf.

Someone pounded on the door.

"He can't be here already." She threw off the covers and scooted to the foot of the bed. "Hold on. I'm coming." Kizzy shoved her feet into her slippers and grabbed her robe. Tying the sash, she stumbled toward the front of the house. She was so not a morning person, and it had to be.... "Five o'clock! You're going to die!" She flung the door open and forgot everything—even the threat of Teter.

"Morning, sunshine." The man from the picture leaned against the frame of her home, grinning at her. "I just wanted to let you know we are setting up camp in your yard." His attention moved from her face down her body, snapping her awake. "I think it best if you don't open the door again in your night clothes," he grumbled, spinning away.

"Excuse me? You're the one who woke me up, so don't even go down that road. Camp where you want, anywhere but the garden." She slammed the door and leaned against it. Her heart was beating fast, and her palms were all sweaty. What was wrong with what she wore? One peek at herself and Kizzy moaned. Her hard nipples could clearly be seen through the robe, not that they were small, nooo. Kizzy had inherited her mother's figure, full and round. Her

6

breast size had always been a problem in school. When the other girls were just starting to develop, Kizzy already had a C cup and growing.

"Men," she grumbled, and moved into her kitchen, which consisted of two cupboards, a small fridge, and stove, and flipped on the coffee. There would be no going back to sleep now that she was up. But, on a good note, the group was here and Kizzy could relax a little. Hopefully, Running Wolf and his men would deter Teter from her doorstep.

"Garden day!" She pumped her fist in the air, excited. Kizzy wouldn't have to worry about Teter coming up behind her when she worked since there were—she peeked out the window—a shocking number of men camping in her yard to stop him. "At least they left a.... What the hell?" Kizzy wrapped her robe tightly around her and stomped to the door, throwing it open again.

All heads lifted, the men's attention now on her, and she knew her cheeks were pink but didn't care. "Could you please not block my truck? I might have to go into town, and I don't want to accidentally run over that bike blocking it." She was about to shut the door when Running Wolf grabbed it, filling the doorway, and she stumbled back.

"I don't want you going into town alone. Until these threats are gone, you will have at least two of us with you if you leave the house, understood?"

"Now, just a minute. I called you to help my friends. That does not give you the right to dictate to me." She stomped her foot and poked his chest with her finger.

He crossed his arms, his feet apart, and gave her one of her father's *really* expressions. "Did my men read the signs wrong? Is Teter not bothering you? My man noticed him earlier here and, from your message, I took it this person was giving you a hard time."

She closed her eyes and let her breath out, knowing he spoke the truth. "No, you are right." Kizzy heard her coffeepot beep, and she needed coffee. "Please come in and have a seat. We might as well compare notes. Coffee?"

Kizzy peeked over her shoulder at him as she reached for a cup. With a quick shake of his head, he said, "We've taken care of the back taxes on the properties you informed me of, and a few of my men have heard that the mayor and this Teter have a fondness for you." He settled at her small table, which made him appear all the larger.

"Teter has been bugging me and going around town telling everyone we are engaged, but the mayor hasn't said boo to me since I showed up here." She poured herself a cup of coffee and inhaled a deep breath of the scent. "Love fresh coffee in the morning." Her gaze met his heated one over the rim of her cup as she burned her tongue, gulping too much at once.

"Damn." She reached for a glass of cold water to soothe the burn. After drinking it all, she remembered something. "Well, there was the dance last year. But Dana, the mayor, danced with everyone." She shrugged, taking in Running Wolf's features. She would love to run her fingers through his long black hair. His dark eyes seemed to take in everything around him, and Kizzy would kill to have high cheekbones like his. "So, do you think they'll give up bugging Lone Star and his family, now that you're here?"

"No, men like that are never happy when we interfere. It will get worse before it gets better. Later today, would you mind introducing us to your friends? Do you really believe he and his people are from the Shawnee tribe?" He stretched his legs out in front of him, seeming to relax a little.

Someone knocked on the door, but Running Wolf beat her to it, pulling it open from where he sat. The man waiting outside wasn't as tall as Running Wolf, but he had shoulder-length hair and wore a black leather vest with no shirt, showing off a six-pack that would make any woman drool. "Kizzy, this is my second-in-command, Sun Bull. If you can't find me, you go to him." Running Wolf shut the door, waving toward the table. "Have a seat, Sun Bull. She's going to tell us what is going on."

"Well, let's see." Kizzy took another sip of coffee, more careful this time, and slipped into the chair Sun Bull pushed a little closer to her. "Okay, um, I've been here for about two years. I bought the land outright before I even arrived. I own something like two acres." She caught herself and took a deep breath. Running Wolf's presence played with not only her hormones but her damn head.

"Okay, first weirdness began when I heard Rose crying, sitting in her garden holding dead plants that would have been food for her family. It was the saddest thing I'd ever seen. Rows and rows of food stomped on and destroyed. The ground was covered in a gas/oil mixture. I helped her and her children shovel what they could into bags and take it to the proper dumping grounds."

"Did you call the police?" Sun Bull asked.

"No, Rose is terrified of the police, and her husband does not want any publicity. It was so sad." Kizzy took a deep breath. "That was also the day I first ran into William Teter."

His woman shivered. He scooted a little closer to reassure her she was safe. "He can't harm you now." He reached out and squeezed her arm. "We will deal with this William Teter." Her phone rang before she could respond.

"Excuse me." Kizzy got up and moved into the other room. Why did she need privacy to answer the phone? Sure, he hadn't known her long, but the unusual circumstances made him edgy.

"What did you find out?" Running Wolf asked his friend.

"Teter is VP of the local bank. Why they want the land, I have no idea yet. The acreage had been sitting empty for years before your woman bought her place and the small group of Shawnee bought theirs. And, yes, they are Shawnee. Raining Tom did some checking, and family lines go back to the right time of their disappearance. But Lone Star's family isn't the only one in the area. There are four other small groups. They have been slowly buying local properties. Maybe Teter found out?"

Kizzy's raised voice carried to them. "William, I am not putting up with this crap. What I do is none of your damn business. If I want twenty men in my damn house, I'll do it, you...." Running Wolf stood and moved into the living room where she glared at the phone in her hand, shaking as if it were a snake. He took it out of her hand and tucked her under his arm, pulling her back to her seat and her coffee.

He lifted the phone to his ear and spoke. "My name is Running Wolf, and you will not be calling here again hassling Kizzy. You have a problem, you will speak with me only. My men and I are not going anywhere anytime soon." He disconnected the line.

Kizzy moaned and plopped down into her chair, reaching for the coffee cup. "Why would you do that? You need to help Rose and Lone Star. I can leave. They invested everything they have in their acreage and some farming equipment, and they don't want to uproot their children again."

"You're not going anywhere, unless you want to. No one is going to drive you away from your land. Now, tell me what else has happened." He pushed her cup toward her.

"Someone in the city raised their taxes. Also, Lone Star and Rose woke up one morning to find their house covered with spray-painted threats. Once, Rose and I were taking her kids to a Halloween thing when a red SUV ran us into the ditch beside the road. We told the cops about that, even the threats in the mail, but Lone Star won't share most of what has happened. He knew the police wouldn't do anything, and he was right. Rose broke down last week and told me she was terrified." She wrapped both hands around the cup and took a deep drink.

"Anything against you personally?" Sun Bull asked.

She tilted her head to the side and put her coffee down. "I really didn't even think about that. I mean, my truck was keyed in town last week. A big scratch down the side. I bank at an out-of-town institution and do everything online to avoid William. Most of the people in town are decent, but there are a few who aren't too friendly." Kizzy got up and moved to the big window, staring outside while sipping her coffee. "And there are others, but they are everywhere, not just here." Kizzy laughed and came back to the table.

"Anyway, I've been planting wild crops around the woods so others won't see, telling Rose where they are. I've also doubled my crop this year. Rose comes over and helps me. But I'm afraid I can't do much more, seems the asses raised my taxes, too. I received a small inheritance when my parents were murdered. I invested it in the stock market and I have to say I did pretty good." She smiled. "But I trusted the wrong person and lost a lot of it. I spent the rest of the money on this house and the new garden. My online store barely brings in enough to keep me going,"

"What do you sell online?" he asked, trying to learn a little more about her.

She moved to a cabinet and opened it, showing him her wares. "I make all my own soaps, shampoos, dried herbs and spices, and different craft things. Mostly, I live off the land, canning my own vegetables and such. My mom taught me a lot before she was killed." She closed the door and poured herself some more coffee.

"You do so much, but don't you get lonely out here?"

"No, I lived in a city. No one stops. Everyone is always in a hurry. I enjoy the quiet. So, tell me about you guys. Why and how did you organize all that you do?" She returned to the table.

"Well, that is my cue to leave." Sun Bull stood and stretched. "I need some sleep since I'll be on guard next." He bowed his head to her. "It was great meeting you, Kizzy, and we'll talk more later."

"What did he mean by his watch?" Kizzy asked.

"You will have a guard on you until this has been sorted out. I have a few men setting up camp over at your friends' house also. As for our story, I'll share that with you tonight. I hope you don't have any plans. I thought we could have a cookout and bonfire? Tell some stories. What are your plans for today?" he asked, standing up.

"Work a little online and in the garden this morning, but I do need to go into town for a few things this afternoon. Rose wanted to go with me. We started sharing rides into town when things got dicey."

"Could you wait till late in the afternoon? I'll take you both, and we'll get what we need for the cookout. My treat, of course."

"No problem with that. Running Wolf, do you believe in dreams?" She followed him toward the front door.

"I do, why? Do you have them?"

Chapter Three

"Five or six years till the dark days are upon us. Would he find his woman and be able to help her in time? Would she accept him?"
Dark Horse, Enforcer, White Buffalo MC

"I've had them since I was a child." She tilted her head to the side. "Sometimes gifts are not welcome, especially when they are things you can't change." Kizzy reached out to pat his arm but stopped herself. "I won't keep you. I know you're tired from the long ride, but I want to say one thing. If I'm hurt or killed, I'd like you to contact my brother. He'll know what to do."

Running Wolf advanced on her, moving so fast she blinked. He cupped her face. "You are not going to die, and, tonight, we will discuss the dream that has you so upset. For now, I leave you with this." He leaned down and placed a small kiss on her lips. "I, too, have been told about you." His expression heated, he took in every inch of her body before coming back up to once more capture her gaze. "There is a connection between us. I knew it when I heard your voice on the answering machine and even more when I was handed a picture of you. We will be exploring it in depth." He kissed her cheek and strode out the door before she could say a word.

"Well, damn," she mumbled. "Sure wasn't expecting that." She moved into her room and grabbed her clothes. She'd wait on the shower until she was done in the garden. Kizzy smiled at the picture hanging to the left of the dresser of her brother and her. She hadn't talked to him in the last two months, she'd been so busy helping Rose.

"Hmm, better call him. My luck, he'll show up here and cause a whole lot of problems." Kizzy grabbed her phone and headed into the bathroom to get dressed.

Ten minutes later, she wished she had never called. Order her to Florida? Who the hell did he think he was? Kizzy grabbed her iPod. Most of the men would be sleeping, but, after the chat with her brother, she needed some music.

She pushed in her earbuds and stepped outside, taking a deep breath. God. She loved the fresh air. Moving around the side of the house, she acknowledged a few men who stood together in the yard with a wave of her hand. No doubt the ones on "guard." She reached down and flipped on her music, humming along.

Yep, digging in the dirt would put her world back on the path of peace. Kizzy opened the door and stepped inside her toolshed, reaching for a hoe. A hand landed on her shoulder. Kizzy jumped and spun, bringing up her knee before she knew who it was.

Running Wolf stepped backward just in time, grunting.

"Don't do that to me." She took out an earpiece then placed her hand on her chest, trying to catch her breath. "Damn. Sorry about that. Natural reflexes kicking in. I didn't hurt you, did I?"

"I was going to suggest you use one earpiece so you can hear someone sneaking up on you." Running Wolf rubbed his chin, staring down at her. "Nice outfit."

"What?" Kizzy wiped her hands on her faded jeans and tank top. "These are my gardening clothes."

"Gardening clothes," he moaned, eyeing her top. "It's a little skimpy, isn't it? You do know I have thirty men here, right? I'd hate to see what you wear when you dress up." He left her to her work.

She grabbed her tools, laughing and already planning on wearing her favorite peasant outfit to the cookout. Maybe not as skimpy, but the lacing made it sexy. Two men peeled off from the group standing by the house and followed her into the woods to her wild garden.

"You might as well tell me your names, so I know who is guarding me," she said.

"I'm Night Song and this is my brother Walking Elk," the taller one said..

Her gaze moved past them and she froze in horror. "Those mother fuckers! I'll fucking burn every single one of their houses," she screamed and dropped her tools, ready to assess the damage, but strong arms pulled her back.

"Don't touch anything till we get pictures and search the area." Running Wolf placed a kiss on her cheek. Where had he come from?

"I'm sorry, Kizzy. We'll get this person, I promise."

She growled. "But that doesn't help all the plants we've lost. I have over six hundred dollars invested in this garden, and it's ruined." Kizzy stomped her foot, clenching her fists. "Shit, this is going to kill Rose. We worked so hard. Sometimes I wish I knew my mom's curses."

Kizzy rushed back to the house and slammed the door behind her, ready to make a list of all the plants she would need to replace. There was no way they would stop her, and her brother could jump in the ocean if he thought she was going to leave her friends. Now they just pissed her off, but —

Her brother's ring tone vibrated in her pocket, and she grabbed the phone.

"Marcus, don't start on me. I have a question. Do you have the box Momma kept under her bed?"

"The really old one?" her brother questioned.

"Yes, that one. It has some of Mom's seeds and some other things I'd like to have. Please send it to the post office box I gave you."

"Come get it yourself," he ordered.

Kizzy peeked over her shoulder. Running Wolf stalked to the doorway, and she waved him inside, continuing her conversation. "What? Marcus, that is blackmail. I told you I'm not coming there. I even have a bodyguard until this mess is over with." She rolled her eyes and held out the phone to Running Wolf. "Tell him you and your men are here so he'll stop acting like a fool." Before he could take it, she jerked it back and yelled, "I swear you'd think I was ten again!" Then she handed Running Wolf the phone and moved into her bedroom, searching for her notebook.

If he hadn't been so furious, he'd be laughing. The way Kizzy dealt with her brother was so cute, but her brother didn't seem to think so. He hollered so loud, it was hard to make out what he said.

"Calm down so I can understand you. My name is Running Wolf."

He let her brother ask all his questions, answering them as best he could. Finally, the man apologized. "I appreciate your being there for my sister even if she's too stupid to know what's best for her."

"I promise you, nothing is going to happen to your little sister and, before you ask, yes, I have a personal interest in her safety and happiness. But that is between your sister and me. I have to go." He hung up the phone. Kizzy returned to his side as he heard a car pull up the drive.

"Shit! Can my day get any worse?" she moaned, opening the door staring at the Jeep.

"Go back inside, Kizzy, and allow me to deal with this man." Running Wolf stepped outside in front of her.

She took a quick peek at the car. "Fine, that I can do because, right now, I don't think I can deal with the weasel." She disappeared inside, shutting the door behind her.

"Kizzy!" the man shouted, stepping out of his car and moving forward.

"Mr. Teter, I do believe you were warned to back off, but let me tell you again. Kizzy does not like you or want anything to do with you. I suggest you get back in your vehicle and leave now."

The short man's face flushed beet-red. "W-who exactly are you?"

Running Wolf leaned forward, his face inches from the man. "I'm her guard and friend. Seems she and her other friends have been having some problems. You wouldn't know anything about those, would you? It might help me when I speak with Frank. Frank Welldon, the state prosecuting attorney? He's coming tonight for our cookout and to help me figure out the tax hike only these people have been dealt." Running Wolf held back a snort when the man paled. Oh yeah, this creep was knee-deep in this shit.

"I have no idea. Kizzy should have told me. I would have researched it. Rest assured I will when I get back to work on Monday. I do have some contacts I can use. If you will excuse me, I forgot about a meeting." Despite his words, he took a step toward Kizzy's door, but Running Wolf blocked his way. After eyeing him, the guy did an about-face and headed toward his car.

"You know they'll just stop until you leave if he's the one doing it," Kizzy said, opening the door.

"No, I think they are on a timeframe for some reason. Things are likely to heat up before we catch them, but the rest of the day should be quiet."

"Do you really know the state prosecuting officer, and why in the world would you tell my brother you were interested in me?" She must have been listening to his conversation.

"Yes, I know Frank, and he'll be here with a few local officials. I informed your brother so he'd know my intentions toward his sister." He focused on her over his shoulder while he listened to the man starting up his car, leaving. Two of Running Wolf's men followed him out of the drive on their bikes.

"My men will help clean up your garden tomorrow, but we really need sleep. Maybe it would be wise to work inside till we go into town later."

Kizzy focused on the road. "Fine. I'll have to call Rose and tell her about what has happened. If she wants to come over here before we go, we can make lists of what we're going to need and, Running Wolf, I haven't agreed to anything yet." She stepped back inside, shutting the door behind her.

He grinned. His Little Gypsy was full of spunk, and she was going to need it before all of this was done, but, in the meantime, he could put some joy into her life. He approached Penn, who sat with his laptop.

Without even moving, Penn said, "Let me guess. You want me to call the local nursery and have plants and soil delivered to replace her garden?"

"Please, but this can be taken out of my personal account. Have them delivered tomorrow morning. It will give the woman something to do while we speak with the other groups of Shawnee."

"I take it you have them coming here?" Penn asked.

"The heads of the families will be here. We'll use her house so they won't be seen if they want to keep hidden for now. I'm going to try and catch a few Zs while she is busy. I have a feeling she's going to keep me moving." He headed for the tent he shared with Sun Bull, hearing Penn's snort.

Chapter Four

"Freedom is a matter of perception my body is free, but my soul cries out for its other half out there waiting to be found."
Running Wolf, President, White Buffalo MC

Kizzy and Rose had worked for two hours making a list of plants and things they would need to start over. They were lucky it was still early in the season and they had plenty of time to plant their second garden. With the things Running Wolf had ordered for her, Kizzy would save a lot of money.

Rose had tried to yell at her for calling in the White Buffalos, but Kizzy had seen the relief in her eyes. In a matter of minutes, she had been hugging her tight and thanking her.

As the two women strolled down the sidewalk of the small town, Rose leaned in and spoke in a low voice. "I think this Running Wolf has a thing for you."

She snorted and took a glimpse behind her. Running Wolf had changed into a pair of black jeans that hugged his butt nicely, and the leather vest he wore with no shirt displayed his hairless chest.

Rose elbowed her as Running Wolf caught her staring. She moaned, wanting to crawl into a hole she was so embarrassed. "Stop," she growled, but Rose only continued to tease her, until the mayor, Dana Sanders, stepped in front of them.

At once. Running Wolf and his friend Dark Horse stepped in front of the two of them, urging them back.

"Is there a problem, Mayor?" Running Wolf asked.

"Who are you?" Dana asked. The mayor was Kizzy's height with grayish-black hair and dead eyes. At least. that was what she called his brown eyes.

"My name is Running Wolf, and I'm here to help some of my friends with a few problems they seem to be having, but I'm sure you know nothing about the damage that has been done to Kizzy's property and her neighbors'."

The mayor inched forward. Dark Horse countered his move, but the mayor's two personal bodyguards moved closer behind him. "This is my town. Remember that." He angled to the side. "Kizzy, you should have come to me. I would have helped. There is no reason to call in outsiders."

Kizzy shuffled past Running Wolf and slid up beside the mayor, bumping into him. "Sorry, but are you going to do something when your own police chief hasn't done crap? Please, I'm not stupid Dana. Maybe now we can find out what you and Teter are really up to. Now, if you will excuse us, we have a garden to replace, since someone decided to destroy mine." Reaching back, she grabbed Rose's hand, and, together, they walked past him.

Running Wolf and Dark Horse moved in behind them. "We'll talk soon, Mayor," Running Wolf said. He turned a stern glare on Kizzy.

"What? Did you really believe I'd say nothing?" she yelled. "Everyone in town knows the mayor has the police chief in his pocket!"

The mayor spun toward her, his eyes bugging out of his head. Running Wolf placed his hand over her mouth, hustling her around the corner before things deteriorated further.

After a moment, Kizzy had enough and kicked him in the shin. Finally, he let her go, glaring at her as he rubbed his leg. "Kizzy!"

"Don't Kizzy me! I'm not a child, and I sure don't like being treated like one. I've known you, what, eight freaking hours, and you act all caveman on me? Take care of yourself, Running Wolf, or I'll make sure I start reading my momma's journal on how to make a damn voodoo doll." Kizzy leaned back. "You know, that might not be a bad idea? Yes!" She knew what she needed to do. "Come on, Rose. I need a few other things on this trip into town." She headed for the craft store, dragging a laughing fool Rose along with her.

"It's not that funny," she mumbled as they got into the store.

"Yes, it was, and you two are perfect for each other." Rose faced the store entrance where Dark Horse and Running Wolf stood. "Already he's thinking of ways to tan your hide for kicking him. I've seen that expression and know it well." Rose shivered.

What the hell was she talking about? "Lone Star never hurt you, did he? Because if he did...."

Rose shook her head. "Oh, girlfriend, do we need to talk. You have led such a sheltered life." Rose proceeded to tell her stories of erotic spankings, bondage, and all sorts of sex toys she had never heard of that had her skin burning red. Spinning around, she almost ran smack into Running Wolf.

He placed his hands on her shoulders and stared down at her. "So what has you so embarrassed? Rose, what kind of stories have you been telling?"

Kizzy reached over, covering her friend's mouth. "Don't you dare."

Rose pushed her hand away. "Oh, just some personal stories, updating my friend on the number of adult things."

"Let the Great Mother open the Earth and swallow me now," Kizzy groaned, never so embarrassed in her life.

***

Running Wolf grabbed onto Kizzy before she could lunge at her friend. "Seems I might have to have a chat with your husband and ask him what kind of stories you could be telling," he teased.

"You wouldn't?" Kizzy asked, wide-eyed.

"Relax, my Little Gypsy. We'll be creating our own stories soon enough." Running Wolf placed a kiss on her ear. "I can't wait to get you back to your home so I can show you what your little outburst earlier gets." He ran his fingers down her back to her ass where he squeezed one of her butt cheeks. "Have you ever had your ass spanked, Little Kizzy?"

She sucked in her breath and tried to push away from him.

His Little Gypsy was excited. Her round nipples were hard. "I bet your panties are wet just thinking of the things I could do to you." He paid her back a little for the bruised shin she'd given him.

"Please."

"A truce?"

She agreed quickly.

"You know you don't really need all of this stuff." He pointed to the items she had gathered. "I don't think you were meant to do this kind of thing. Maybe that's why your mother didn't teach you her curses?"

"Guess I'm not much of a gypsy." She sighed. "Marcus and my cousins have been so protective of me. I'm sorry about kicking you, but that man makes me so mad."

Running Wolf tweaked her nose. "I want you to let us take care of the mayor and the banker, okay?"

"I still want to try the doll." She pulled a few pieces of hair along with a small pair of scissors from her pocket. "I do have some talents my cousin Turtle taught me."

"How did you get close enough to cut that?" Running Wolf touched the chunk of hair in her hand. "You know he's going to miss that much hair."

She shrugged. "How is he going to know it was me?"

The door to the fabric shop banged open, and he stepped in front of Kizzy as Dark Horse did the same with Rose.

"You little witch! Where is my hair?" The mayor stomped toward them, followed by the chief of police.

"I have no idea what you mean." Kizzy peeked around Running Wolf.

"Search her right now, Chief!" the man yelled.

"No one is touching Kizzy, Mr. Mayor, and if your thug knows what's good for him, he'll back off. I'm sure Frank would love to hear about how a police chief harassed a woman," Running Wolf said.

"Frank who, and you are?" the cocky chief got up close and personal to him.

"Oh, I'm sure you've heard of Frank Welldon. Matter of fact, I'll be meeting him later tonight. Would you like to join us? I'm sure he would love to meet you," Running Wolf stepped back, his attention now centered on Kizzy.

"Watch your step, Ms. Kizzy. They won't be around forever," the cop said. "Let's go, Mayor. I have work to do, not trying to figure out where a chunk of your hair went."

Letting the cop walk out of the shop was a testimony to his patience, especially since the man had just threatened what was his. Anger radiated from Dark Horse as well. "We do this by the book for now, but if it does not work, we'll see," Running Wolf told his enforcer who just snorted.

"Get your stuff. We have work to do," Running Wolf told Kizzy, and she rushed around gathering what she needed, but her hands shook as she reached for a number of things, dropping a few items in the process. His Little Gypsy was not one for violence. She had a pure heart, and he was going to make sure she stayed that way.

Taking her bag of things, Running Wolf stepped outside before the women to find a few more of his men there waiting for them. He lifted his eyebrow.

Dark Horse shrugged. "There is no sense in risking your woman. She gives us hope for the Dark Times coming."

"What Dark Times? What does that mean?" Kizzy asked, following him.

"In time, I'll explain, but for now, let's deal with this personal problem first, shall we?" He lifted the bag in his hand. "So do you think you can do this?"

"I wish I'd gotten close enough to the cop to get hair from him as well, but I don't have the balls to go that far," she mumbled. "The mayor and Teter are a different story."

"And how will you know if it's working?" Running held the door open to the nursery for them. His men were already in the place.

A small woman approached them, fidgeting and peering over her shoulder. "Kizzy I'm so, so sorry about what happened, but I'm afraid I don't have what you need here."

"What? The tomato plants right over there?" Kizzy pointed to her left. "The herbs down farther?" Kizzy did a slow circle, scanning their surroundings. "Oh, I see. Should have known. Don't worry, Lisa. I know you have to make a living. I'll just order from a different place. But you make sure you use that ointment for your husband." She patted the woman's arm then swung around and moved back outside followed by Rose and the rest of her entourage.

"I'm going to help you make those damn dolls. I've had enough. The nerve to threaten that poor old lady," Rose snapped. "It's time this Indian brought out her war bonnet."

"What happened in there?" Running Wolf asked.

"Teter was in there with his goons. I'm pretty sure they were threatening Lisa's husband if she were to sell us anything." Kizzy headed straight toward her SUV.

"Wait, how do you know when we didn't notice anything?" Running Wolf asked.

"Because you haven't seen all the men Teter has working for him, but we have." Kizzy took Rose's hand. "We could drive over to Oberlin. They have a few nurseries there no one from here can control. Matter of fact, I know the owner of the one. I'll call him when we get in the car."

Running Wolf stopped them. "Wait, should we go back and help her?"

She shook her head. "You might help her for now. But as soon as you leave, they'll take it out on her disabled husband. It's best to go somewhere else for now." Kizzy placed her hand on his chest. "Look, I want to help her, too, but we'd do more damage if we go barging in there."

"I could just kill Teter's men and get this over with, but she's right. We can't cover the whole town. I have a feeling these two men and their thugs have their hands dipped into a lot of different things around here. You believed I wanted to leave her, that I didn't want to help her."

Rose pointed a finger at him. "I'll have you know this woman not only saved my son's life, she has helped a number of these city people. If you even think that, you are not the man for my friend. Come on, Kizzy, you can stay with us tonight since I know the dickhead will come by after that show in the fabric shop."

"You mean the cop? Why would he come over? Especially since we're there to make sure nothing bad happens?" Running Wolf asked.

"Because Kizzy used to date the asshole until she found out what a jackass he was," Rose said. "He's been trying to get her back."

Chapter Five

"Her skin is as soft as the petals of a flower, and when she turns that smile on me my soul blooms seeking her light." Running Wolf, President, White Buffalo MC

Running Wolf's expression of disbelief only made her more furious. Who the hell was he to judge her anyway? She hooked her arm around Rose's and moved forward, ignoring the men altogether.

"My life is none of their concern, Rose, so let's just drop the subject. They are here to help you and your family. I can pack up and leave anytime. Did I tell you Marcus wants me to come down and live near him?" She took a deep breath and let it out. "Maybe it's time I think of moving on anyway. My mom might have been right."

Rose stopped, glaring at her. "No, she was not. You are doing fine. It's not your fault we have dickheads around here. True, your family protected and sheltered you, but never doubt yourself. You've accomplished so much already. Just what you did for me is impressive." Rose hugged her tight. "If not for you, I would have given up long ago. You've kept us all going and fighting for what is right. So do not even think of giving up. Who would show me the rest of those dances you promised to teach me?"

Kizzy giggled. "Okay, but tonight we show your husband how much you've learned, deal?"

"Not unless you are going to do it with me."

"Of course. Payback's a bitch, don't you think?" Kizzy reached over and squeezed her arm.

Rose spoke close to her ear. "I take it we're going to wear the outfits you made for us?"

"Yep, might as well do the whole thing. What do you think?" She peeked back, noticing Running Wolf speaking to Dark Horse.

"Oh, honey, he has no idea what is coming his way, and you are right, payback is a bitch. We'll be over at seven tonight. My folks should be able to keep an eye on the kids because, after our dance, well, you know." Rose fanned herself.

"Come on, hot woman, we have work to do. Tomorrow, I will be planting a new garden if I have to drive down to Oberlin myself and get those plants."

Running Wolf took her hand, twining his fingers in hers. "That won't be necessary. I called Penn with your list of plants and he is having them delivered tomorrow morning, so you two will have plenty to keep you busy. I have to apologize for earlier," he continued. "I'm afraid I let a little bit of jealousy get in my way when I had no right, at least yet."

"What do you mean yet? I haven't agreed to anything and this is the second time you've indicated that there was something going on between us—"

Without warning, Running Wolf tackled her onto the sidewalk.

"*Oof!*" It seemed as if her lungs had left her body.

The whine of bullets buzzed past them. Running Wolf covering her body was not helping her breathe, but he'd thrown his arms around her head, keeping her skull from hitting the concrete.

"Are you okay?" He lifted her and carried her into the dry cleaners next to them, surrounded by his men—she hadn't even known any of the others had come with them.

He patted her body for damage while she took a big gasp of air. "Where is Rose?"

"Right there with Dark Horse. Where does it hurt?"

"I'll be bruised for a while, but I'm okay now that I can breathe. What the hell happened?" Kizzy tried to see outside the door they had come in.

"Sniper. Anyone hurt in here?"

"The owner took a bullet in the arm," a woman yelled from behind the counter; Kizzy knew that voice. "He's bleeding like a stuck pig,"

"Maggie, you okay?" Kizzy asked.

The woman popped into view. "Yeah, but I'll be sore tomorrow. That big lug landed on me. What the hell happened?"

"Whoever it was got away. We found the gun, but the police chief took it. He'll be here in a few seconds," Sun Bull stated. "You okay, Kizzy?"

She waved at him, but, all of a sudden, her legs started to shake, so Kizzy slid down the wall to sit. "I think I'll rest right here. Maybe you can just get the car."

Rose settled beside her. "I second that idea. I think I've had enough excitement for the day," Rose mumbled, just as the dickhead chief of police entered the building.

***

Running Wolf and Dark Horse faced off with the chief of police.

"I'll need to speak with the two ladies," he said.

"No you won't. We were all out there. The four of us can each give you a statement, but you will not get any closer to the women, and you know why."

"Are they okay?" Tack asked, stepping into the store.

"They just want to go home," Running Wolf said.

"Give me a few minutes." Tack addressed the chief of police. "Maxim, I will personally question everyone. Frank Welldon is waiting for you outside. Oh, and not to worry. I've already taken the weapon from your men who seemed determined to put their damn prints all over it. We'll be discussing retraining some of your men real soon, that is, if you are still wearing that uniform."

The man sputtered, his face flaming. "You should have stayed with me, Kizzy. I could have protected you." He stormed out of the store.

They needed to get both women back where they would be protected. As soon as Maxim left, he knelt in front of them. "He's not going to touch you, either of you. We'll protect you," Running Wolf said, but the Kizzy faced away from him.

"May I?" Tack asked, kneeling next to him.

Running Wolf moved out of the way, but stayed close. "Kizzy, Rose, this is my friend Tack. He's with the state police and is helping out here. You can trust him. He won't hurt you."

Tack took over, asking questions in a way that drew the ladies out without frightening them.

He stood, dusting his pant knees. He'd never been so pissed off. Dark Horse stepped up to him. "Sky Fox and I will check out the car."

"Good. I want to move out of here as soon as we can."

After Dark Horse and Sky Fox left, a pair of paramedics entered.

As they checked over the women, Dark Horse waved Sun Bull over.

"We have problems." Sun Bull's words had him cringing. "They tried to fire bomb her home. She's lucky we were there to stop them. Tack has two of the thugs already locked up, but it's escalating faster than we believed it would. I have men scouting around and have set up a two-mile perimeter around her house and Rose's. No one will get in without our knowing.

"I've called in the second team. We're going to need them since it's obvious this is more than two men we are dealing with."

Dark Horse pulled Kizzy's SUV up to the curb. "Agreed. Let everyone know we'll be moving." Running Wolf held out a hand to Kizzy. "Ready to go home?"

"More than you know." She tried to get up and flinched, sitting back on her butt. "Damn that hurt."

"Shit." He leaned down and carefully lifted his woman up in his arms.

"What are you doing?" Kizzy struggled then subsided with a moan.

"Hold still. You're most likely bruised from me falling on you, but, just in case, I'll have Red Hawk examine you as soon as we get you both safely away from here. Rose, your husband will meet us at Kizzy's, with the children." He led the way outside and ran to the car.

He opened the back door to the SUV and helped the women inside. "Thank you, Dark Horse. Have Red Hawk meet us at Kizzy's house. I think I bruised her ribs."

"I'm fine. Just a little sore. A hot bath and I'll be fine."

"I want to make sure. I think we're going to keep you at home till this is over with. Rose, you and the children will have to stay inside, unless we are with you. Are the children out of school yet for summer?" He climbed into the front seat as Dark Horse started the car, while Sun Bull and three of his other men pulled in front of them with their hogs.

Rose murmured, "So much for dancing tonight."

"We'll dance. I need to. Maybe it will help everyone loosen up and have a good time. Just forget for a few minutes." Kizzy lifted her head, her eyes meeting his. "We all have been through much today."

"Did Sun Bull tell you about Soaring Eagle?" Dark Horse asked him.

He stiffened. "What happened? Did he travel to the other world?" The man had been his mentor and friend for so long.

"He's here, back at Kizzy's place."

"What? How? Last I heard he was in Virginia. Is he okay? Who the hell allowed him to come?" If he got shot or hurt here, all hell would break loose. They didn't need the extra attention.

"You know better than that, and he rode his horse here. The two assigned to him couldn't get him to go back, so they rode with him." Dark Horse snorted with a little grin on his face, which was a rare thing. "That is one man I respect. He never lets anyone stop him."

Running Wolf frowned. "Have I stopped you from doing something?"

"No, and if you had tried, I would have been gone long ago. But the past always has a way of showing up."

"Isn't that the truth? Soaring Eagle was the one who asked me to come to you, and he was right. You have done well. Thank you for everything." Running Wolf squeezed his friend's shoulder. "Anytime you need help, ask. I will back you in anything. I trust you that much."

Dark Horse's hands tightened on the steering wheel, his knuckles going white. "The same goes for me." He indicated the backseat. "No one will hurt your woman as long as I'm around."

Why would Soaring Eagle come all this way to be with him? Maybe a vision. The last time he had one, he'd taken off.

Chapter Six

"Even when there seems to be no hope, a beam of light shines, and mine is Kizzy, my future wherever it leads." Running Wolf, White Buffalo MC

Kizzy sat forward in the backseat, her ribs still aching. A row of horses was hitched to her shed, many of the riders dressed as if in the old days. "Wow, impressive."

"I didn't call in half of these men. I'm afraid our medicine man, Soaring Eagle, must have," Running Wolf replied. "He is like a father to all of us and has visions that often come true."

She sat back slowly. "I'm afraid I don't have much food, but your medicine man is welcome to take my bed. I can sleep on the sofa by the window." Kizzy ran her hand through her hair. "I usually end up falling asleep there reading, anyway. Plus, he's older and should have a comfortable bed for however long he is here."

Dark Horse shut the car off, looking in the rearview mirror at her. "You would do this for him, even though you don't know him?"

"I was raised to respect my elders and I know this man is important to you all. How can I not offer this when you have already done much for us?" She reached over and squeezed Dark Horse's arm.

Warmth spread up her arm till the vision was upon her. A tall woman, with dark-blonde hair stared at the farm, tears running down her bruised face. Off to the right, a man was being hauled away in a cop car as an ambulance pulled up.

"Kizzy, damn it, girl, snap out of it." Rose's arms wrapped around her. "You okay? You were crying."

"Bring your woman out of the car. She'll be tired. I have a

28

feeling Dark Horse has his new destination coming." An older man she thought might be Soaring Eagle moved toward the bonfire in the middle of the yard.

"How long was I out of it?" Kizzy asked. Rose released her and slipped out of the car.

"You were out about fifteen minutes, and I have to say you scared the living crap out of me, Little Gypsy," Running Wolf growled as he carefully lifted her and pulled her out of the car.

She took a deep breath, loving the scent of an open fire. Tears filled her eyes as she remembered the last time she had been at a bonfire. Both her parents had been alive. Family had been everywhere that night. Songs had been sung into the early morning, and they'd danced until Kizzy had been so tired her father had ordered her to bed.

"What's wrong?" Running Wolf asked.

"Just remembering the last time I was with my family. We had a big celebration sort of like this. The bonfire flames seemed to reach the stars that night."

"Your father is an honorable man. I spoke with him recently. It's one of the reasons I'm here and why your brother is also." Her brother was indeed there; he must have arrived while they were gone.

"Are you okay?" Mason asked.

"I'm fine, just a little sore. What are you doing here?"

"Father came to me a few nights ago. It seems our family is to join with the White Buffalos' men." Her brother's brow creased, his expression when trying to concentrate. "Something about preparing, getting everyone ready. I have no idea what he meant."

"I do," Soaring Eagle said. "Please tell your family to join us, and I'll tell you what I know. They are lingering in the woods. But first, Two Eyes, get the food started and set up our tents. We'll be staying for a few days."

"You are welcome to have my room, sir. I have a specially made sofa bed in my window I can use," Kizzy offered.

The old man shook his head. "No, child, I will sleep under the stars for the rest of my time on this Earth, but thank you for thinking of me. Now I do believe your man was going to have Red Hawk check you over. This would be a good time to do that while everyone gets organized."

"But I'm fine, just a little sore," she protested.

As if she hadn't spoken, Running Wolf cradled her in his arms and carried her to the house, followed by her brother. Inside, another man waited.

"That is Red Hawk. He served as a medic in Iran for two years," Running Wolf explained.

"Are you a mind reader, too?"

"No just very observant." He placed a gentle kiss on her head. "I take care of what's mine, and you are mine even if you are not ready for that yet." He set her on her sofa in the window.

"I'm really better now," she said.

Red Hawk knelt next to her.

"Why don't you lie down so I can make sure?"

"I always was a sucker for a handsome man," she grumbled but obeyed.

"No, you just have a big heart and hard time telling anyone no," her brother shot back.

She ignored his comment. "So who came with you? Please tell me Uncle Stefan is...." Kizzy lifted her head to see all three of her uncles coming inside. "Ugh," she moaned at the slight pain when Red Hawk ran his hand over her left side.

"You are bruised, but nothing is broken. Just take it easy for the next few days. No lifting."

She snorted. "It must be taught to you as children, because I swear my brother and uncles get the same expression on their face." She patted his arm as he helped her sit up. Her brother and uncles were all staring at Running Wolf.

"Damn this is going to get ugly," she muttered.

"Not to worry, our boss can handle himself." Red Hawk winked and moved to the door. "Have fun boss," he waved at Running Wolf.

"Okay, have at it, gentlemen, because I'm not backing down. She's mine," he declared.

"Do you have a freaking death wish?" She tried to get up.

"Stay put," all three of her uncles ordered at once.

"Excuse me. This is my home." She pushed to her feet and joined Running Wolf.

Running Wolf glanced down at his Little Gypsy. "You should have stayed put. You're hurting. I'm sure your family and I can talk without resorting to violence. You've been through enough today." He wrapped his arm around her and placed a kiss on her cheek. "Why don't you go soak in the tub. It might help, and we'll be gentlemen. There is nothing for you to worry about."

She glared at her family. "Do not pull any shit. He saved my life today."

One of her uncles stepped up to her and cupped her cheek. "Kizzy, I promise we will not harm your man, but we do need to speak with him. Now, go take your bath and stop worrying."

"Fine, but if I hear one thing breaking, and that includes his bones, I swear I'll find my mom's curse book and make sure each of you has to live on the damn toilet. This does not mean I'm going for all this claiming crap either. I just don't want to have your blood all over the place. And watch it, Running Wolf. They like to bury my male friends in the group up to their necks. They did it once before."

"Hey now, that idiot hurt you," Mason said.

"Well behave." She paused to grab a garment bag from her room then disappeared into the bathroom.

Her uncles said nothing. The sound of the shower running came from behind the closed door. "So you say our niece is yours. Why? Oh, my name is Stephan, I'm the oldest. That is my brother Ares, the youngest, and Santana."

Running Wolf acknowledged each man and moved over to the sofa by the window. "Please sit. This will take a little bit." He waited for the four men take seats around him.

For the next twenty minutes, Running Wolf explained what his group of warriors did and why.

Stephan sat forward. "That does not explain why you believe my niece is your woman."

"No, it does not. Our Great Mother has given each of my warriors a talent. Red Hawk's gift is healing, and not only with medicine. He can heal by touch, but it takes a lot out of him. Our elder, Soaring Eagle, has had been sent messages, visions about life, people, all of which have come to pass. One such message was about the women that would stand beside me and my warriors. Remember, we not only help our people but prepare them for something what is coming. We would need strong women beside us who could travel and also help. We experienced signs the old medicine man mentioned: my heart was beating fast, and peace settled over me the first time I heard her voice. I've never been possessive of anyone or anything until now. No one shall harm her."

Stephan sat back. "My brother was right. You will be perfect for our Little Butterfly, but be warned. She has a heart of gold and people swarm to her for help. Even as a child, she drew strangers to her. It's another reason why she is so special to us all. Tonight, you'll witness firsthand what we are talking about."

Running Wolf was about to ask what he meant when Kizzy stepped out of the bathroom and every thought left him. Her uncles stood up. "We'll meet you outside. And you, young lady, do not overdo it tonight. Your cousins knew you would want to sing and dance." Stephan hugged Kizzy and left them alone.

She stepped forward and bells jingled, her skirt the colors of the earth and sky. Kizzy wore no shoes but had rings on her toes, ankle, and arm bracelets of gold and silver. She wore no rings on her hands except one on her index finger.

Kizzy was covered in all the right places, but the ensemble still had him hard as a bull in a rutting frenzy. "What are you doing?" He placed his hands on the soft bare skin above where her skirt rode low on her hips. A tattoo peeked out on each hip, trailing toward the back. "Later tonight, I will show you my world. I have a feeling we are going to need something to liven things up after the news Soaring Eagle gives us."

She rested her hands on his chest and stared up at him. "I heard what you said, and I'm not running away, but I will be romanced before I commit to you." She stood on her toes and kissed his chin. "Now, let's go hear this news."

Chapter Seven

"Her dancing should be outlawed, but her movements had me squirming in my seat, wanting, no needing to get up and dance with her." Running Wolf, President, White Buffalo MC

Kizzy hid her smile as Running Wolf grumbled and wrapped an arm around her, glaring at his men who whistled and hooted at her as they exited her home.

Rose winked at her as they all gathered around the fire. Kizzy was going to sit on the ground, but Running Wolf pulled her into his lap, nipping at her neck. "No one's getting near you."

When Soaring Eagle stood, staring into the fire, the levity faded. The only sounds were the popping of the fire and the breeze soughing through the night forest around them. Even the stars seemed to dull waiting for the story to be told.

He held a pipe in his hand. "Our timetable has been set. The greed and destruction of our Earth has come to a head. Already, Mother Earth and the great spirits from above have moved to fight back to save our world." Soaring Eagle walked around the fire to the north taking a puff of smoke.

"The north winds hide the place we must go to." He glanced over at Running Wolf. "Canada, British Columbia, in the mountains, there you will find the first safe zone for us. That is where you and a quarter of your men will go and start preparing for our people. The volcanoes in that area are cooling. Mother Earth is pulling the fire from there." Soaring Eagle moved to the west side of the fire and took another puff of the pipe.

"On the west side, we'll need someone to go to Central Valley, California. There I see some kind of underground something. It will lead down into the Earth. Under the sea is the next place for us to stabilize." Soaring Eagle moved to south side of the fire and took another puff from the ancient-looking pipe.

"On the south side, it will be Cusseta Mountain, Douglassville, Texas." Soaring Eagle's attention slid to Dark Horse. "This is where you go and, yes, you are ready. Running Wolf's woman will inform you about your woman there." Soaring Eagle slowly moved to the east side, completing his circle.

"Maine, Old Speck Mountain. Oxford County is where Two Eyes will go with his band of men, and don't give me that crap about guarding me." Soaring Eagle sat down and passed the long ceramic pipe to Running Wolf.

Running Wolf closed his eyes and said a prayer before taking a puff then handed the pipe to Dark Horse.

"How long do we have?"

"Five years, maybe six, but rest assured, warriors, you will meet your ladies before the darkness comes." Soaring Eagle focused on her. "Your father visited me the other night. It seems your family will be coming on our journey with us. He was warning me about something, but one minute he was there and the next something dark slipped into my vision. That hasn't happened for a long time. Something else is coming after her; we must protect her."

Her brother hissed. "Could it be family?"

"Mason, sit down," Uncle Stephan ordered. "We all knew something wasn't right when your parents were murdered . Any clues at all. Soaring Eagle?"

"I'm sorry, but all that was shown to me was the warning."

"We'll be ready. Do we know what will happen in five to six years?" Running Wolf asked.

"No, just be ready. We will be given signs as it was written long ago. Now, enough of this sadness. I do believe we were promised some music?"

Kizzy patted Running Wolf's hand and stood but was shocked to see her three favorite dancing partners coming from the back. "Damn it, Stephan you didn't tell me my cousins had come."

"Do you really think we'd allow them out of our sight until we knew the situation? The others will be here tomorrow."

Kizzy hugged her cousins Reba, Shantel, and Nicky and introduced Rose to them while they started to stretch. She looked over her shoulder at Ares with the sax and mouthed, "Abraxas."

He threw his head back and laughed.

She took a deep breath, allowing the music to take her away from everything. The music, the sax, drum, guitar were all her dance partners tonight under the stars. Dancing for the man who claimed she was his.

She was stiff, at first. It had been a long time since Kizzy had danced for an audience, and tonight she really wanted to impress one man. Her bells added to the melody. The four women moved around the fire like fireflies, each giving her own performance.

Swaying her feet, hands, and hips, the words she sang following her body movements, Kizzy let it all out. Her family echoed her song, which drifted to the stars and moon above. Showing her love for the night, she wound herself around Running Wolf, touching him.

From the heated expression on Rose's face, she and her husband wouldn't be staying long. As the music reached its peak, pain exploded in her shoulder. She stumbled and dropped to the ground.

"Dark Horse!" Running Wolf yelled.

"We're on it!"

Running Wolf lifted her from the dirt and carried her toward the house.

"Remind me to curse the person who did this," Kizzy grumbled. "We didn't get to finish our song."

When he set her on the kitchen table, she noticed blood dripping onto her outfit. "I'll freaking kill them. Give me that towel before it ruins my skirt."

"Put her on the sofa, Running Wolf, and get her a towel so we can cover her up while I work on her," Red Hawk ordered, moving her hand away from the wound. "Running Wolf will buy you a new outfit."

"My mother made it for me." Her voice cracked, and tears filled her eyes.

"Not to worry, Little Butterfly. Your aunt Nella will clean it. You know she can get anything out of clothes." Stephan patted her shoulder.

"But can she fix the hole?" Kizzy slumped, unconscious.

"What hole? Did she get shot twice?" Running Wolf handed Red Hawk the towel as he stripped her top off and started to work on her.

"Yes," Red Hawk, said digging in his bag. "Be grateful she has passed out because this is going to hurt. Hold her shoulders down, Running Wolf. I don't need her moving around."

Running Wolf held onto his woman as his friend dug the bullets out and cleaned the wounds on her shoulder and upper chest. There were no words to describe the feelings he had right now. He had never been so angry.

If Dark Horse found the person who did this, there would be nothing left of them. When she was bandaged and ready, Running Wolf carefully lifted, Kizzy and carried her to her room, tucking the blanket around her. Tonight, he would sleep with his woman. No one would touch what was his again.

"You, my Little Gypsy, are not going to like the guards on you, but until we leave this place, you will not be alone again." He placed a kiss on her lips. "Rest and know I'm here for you."

One of her cousins, he couldn't remember her name, followed them in and laid a hand on his arm. "Please allow us to get her out of her dress so we can fix it for her."

"Just don't move her upper body." He took advantage of the free moment to return to the living area and check in with his men.

"In the morning, I will bring an herbal tea to help with the pain and keep infection away. Try and keep her in bed tomorrow," Red Hawk said.

"Good luck with that," her brother said.

"She will listen to me, or I'll spank her cute little butt." Running Wolf shook Red Hawk's hand. "Thank you for everything. Go rest. I know you did more than you were supposed to."

"It had to be done or she would have had to be taken to the hospital, and I know how much you hate them," Red Hawk explained.

Dark Horse stood in the open doorway, holding a woman by the arm and holding a black ops tactical weapon. "Here is your shooter."

"What are you doing with my wife?" Ares moved toward the woman, but Running Wolf stepped in front of him.

"She's the one who shot Kizzy."

"What? Are you out of your mind? Betsy would never...." Ares peeked around him. "Tell him Betsy."

"Tell him what? I did it, and if I hadn't gotten bitten by a damn bug as I fired, she would be dead. She should have died with her parents, but, no, the bitch had to take off on a trip." The woman struggled then subsided. "Do you know how much control that bitch and her family had over us? Any word her father said was law, and you followed like a puppy. Not to mention the whole family babied that bitch in there. You put her up on a pedestal and treated our kids like dirt. If you'd let that pervert take her, half of the problem would have been solved."

The bedroom door opened to reveal Kizzy, supported by two of her cousins, tears running down her cheeks.

"You killed Momma and Papa?" Her lips trembled.

Running Wolf clenched his fists. "Call in Tack. I won't kill a woman, but she can sit behind bars for the rest of her life."

"There is no need. The Great Mother has taken it upon herself to call this one back," Soaring Eagle said from behind Dark Horse.

Running Wolf tried to get Kizzy back to bed, but she refused. "Sofa, please," she begged.

"As long as you don't move around." He settled her among the cushions, careful of her injured shoulder. "What do you mean there's no need?" Then he knew. "The bug bite."

"Yes, she won't last long. It would seem we have one of our signs. It has started," Soaring Eagles confirmed.

Red blisters appeared on Betsy's face, arms, and hands.

"I swear there is something moving in those bubbles." Dark Horse backed up, shivering. "Spiders."

"Not to worry. They won't touch us," Soaring Eagle said. Ares stepped forward, but Soaring Eagle lifted his staff, blocking him. "You know in your heart she was never connected to you. She is getting what she deserves. Your children will need their father. But not to worry, another will come before the dark time and heal your heart."

"Uncle Ares?" Kizzy patted the sofa next to her as Betsy fell to the floor, clutching her throat.

Ares knelt in front of Kizzy. "I'm so sorry, Little Butterfly, so sorry. My own brother. She killed my brother."

Kizzy ran her fingers through his hair. "I knew all of you kept an eye on me. I heard Papa talking to Stephan about how he worried about crazy people attacking me." Kizzy rested her head on the back of the sofa and closed her eyes. "I hated knowing I was different. Even in school, poor Mason had to guard me. Maybe it would have been better if one of them had gotten me. At least you would have your brother."

"No! Do you know how hard they tried for you? Your momma wanted a girl so badly. She lost two babies before she conceived you." Ares took her hand. "You were her world and ours. Our family had been torn apart for years before you were born. But we were all there for the birth of every child. When you were born, a peace settled over us. Whatever we were fighting about before seemed so petty. After that, we knew you were special and weren't about to let anything happen to you."

"He's right, you know," Soaring Eagle said. "The group that will follow you will be the largest. With Running Wolf's strength and your ability to calm those around him, you will be a major asset to our people and yours. Look at Dark Horse. The man hates spiders, but he still stands there, guarding the door without shaking. I could feel it the moment you arrived. You were born to be with Running Wolf, Kizzy. It's your destiny."

"Well, this Little Gypsy is going to bed, and you will sleep. We don't want to mess up all the healing work Red Hawk did." Running Wolf lifted Kizzy carefully into his arms but paused, facing the door. "Dark Horse?"

"She is gone. I'm going to have nightmares."

Kizzy shook her head. "You will not have dreams of spiders, but dreams of your new woman. Know her, Dark Horse, because she will need you."

She slumped in Running Wolf's arms after her proclamation, and he shifted her higher. "Let's go, Little Gypsy. No more helping. You need rest."

"Do you mind?" Her brother held out his hands. "I'd like to spend a little time with her. Plus, I believe you have some things you need to take care of?"

"I'll be in there in a little bit." Running Wolf placed a kiss on her head. "You will stay with her till I get back?"

Mason nodded.

Placing her into his arms was the hardest thing he had done, but they had things to do, and one of them was to start planning their trip north.

Chapter Eight

"Her anger is like that of a chili pepper, but so is her passion once he touches the fire of her." Running, Wolf President White Buffalo MC

Kizzy pulled the pillow over her head, sobbing as soon as her brother laid her on the bed and closed the door. The bed dipped as Mason lay down next to her.

"Kizzy, you know this isn't your fault. Uncle Ares always did have trouble with his wife. It's not news she was bonkers."

"Momma and Papa would still be living if not for me." She lifted the pillow off her face and stared up at him. "How can you stand to be in the same room with me? I took them away from you."

He lowered his head until his nose was almost touching hers and glared at her. "No, you did not. That bitch out there did this. About a week before Momma and Papa were killed, Papa came to me. Seems Momma had one of her visions. They knew something was coming, and he made me promise to stay close to you. He asked this of his brothers, too. I think Momma knew about this dark time or whatever they are calling it." Mason put a kiss on her cheek.

Kizzy rolled onto her side and groaned, remembering her injury. "Fuck. I hate this. Mason, how can we choose who comes with us? Is it wrong? Do we warn others? What if no one believes us?" Kizzy twined her fingers with his. "So many questions. I have no idea where we would even start. Do we stay here or just start packing up to head to this place?"

"We have time, and the rest of our family will be here in the next few days. I've sent for Rona and the kids. Did I tell you Storm lost his first tooth and Mae has been practicing her dancing? She says I have to help Aunt Kizzy." He smiled and peeked at his sister. "You should see her move, Kizzy. She reminds me so much of you when you were smaller."

"I've missed the little munchkins." She squeezed her brother's hand. "Go on, now. I know you have things to do to help our uncles. I'll be fine." She wanted some time alone.

"Only if you promise me you'll call if you need me. We have to stick together now. I can't lose you." Her brother got off the bed, staring down at her. "I look at you sometimes and I see Momma. The way you laugh and dance. I'll kill anyone that hurts you Kizzy. Even family."

Mason shut the door behind him. He would follow up on his promise, too, but it wasn't right. Her family shouldn't have to feel like they needed to protect her, or that she couldn't be out there alone. Their concern always made her feel like a failure, as if she could do nothing right without help.

Kizzy hugged her pillow, tears slowly running down her cheeks. "I'm sorry Momma, Papa." She closed her eyes, all of a sudden so tired.

Strange plants. Light shone down from above. Kizzy had no idea where it was coming from or where the hell she was. She did a complete circle, taking everything in around her. Was this a dream or a vision?

She stood on some kind of ledge overlooking an underground forest. A river ran through it, and Kizzy could actually hear birds and animals. But then the picture changed. She was riding behind Running Wolf on his bike. Dark Horse, next to them, was followed by at least a hundred of Running Wolf's men. They came upon a street sign: Entering Douglassville, Texas.

Again, the vision changed, and Kizzy sucked in her breath. The woman had visited her visions before, but this time Kizzy recognized the threat. This biker gang was a nasty bunch. They were called the Irons, and when they visited a town, they trashed it, murdered people, and worse....

The president of the club smiled right at her, grabbing his crotch.

"No!" She jerked up, moaning at the pain in her shoulder.

"Easy there, Little Gypsy." Running Wolf wrapped his arms around her. "You're soaking wet. What's wrong?"

A chill ran down her spine to her toes. Kizzy was so scared. She had witnessed some of the damage the Irons had done. Her family had always stayed away, but it would seem they were going right into the den of them.

"Have you heard of the Irons?" She was almost afraid to say the name.

Running Wolf stiffened. "I know of them, why?"

"Because it would seem we're going to be running into them real soon in Texas. I've seen pictures of the president of that club—talk about scary—but nothing in comparison to what I just dreamed." She peeked at the clock. Seven o'clock in the morning and it felt as if she just had lain down. It was going to be a very long day, especially since it was obvious they all were going to be packing up soon. But, first, she needed a shower in the worst way.

She flipped back the covers and started to inch toward the edge of the bed, but Running Wolf wrapped his arm around her waist.

"Where are you going Little Gypsy?" He kissed the side of her neck. "It's early, and I, for one, was hoping we could talk for a little while before being interrupted." He nipped the top of her shoulder.

"Are you sure you want to talk?" She giggled.

His gaze met hers. "Unfortunately, you are not healed enough for our loving to take place yet, baby, but soon." He carefully laid her back, towering over her. "But I would glimpse what is mine, if you would allow me?" His hand ran up her thigh until he came to the bottom of her shirt.

"Am I yours, Running Wolf?" She closed her eyes as tears threatened to fall. "Last week I was wondering where my life was going. I was thinking of moving, needing something." She opened her eyes. "Why do I feel like my life isn't my own anymore?"

He leaned down and kissed her lips softly. "Because it's not. Our lives are now twined together. There is no you or me, just us. My soul, my heart will never be alone again." Running Wolf unbuttoned her nightshirt and spread it open.

The heat in his eyes was a relief. She released the breath she had been holding and reached up, running her finger down his check. "You amaze me. So many depend on you, yet you make sure I'm safe and well even though we just met."

"We might have just met, but I believe we were once joined. My connection to you is so deep it feels as if I've known you for a long, long time."

"I hear you in there."

"Kizzy, if you don't want to be embarrassed, be out here in five minutes." Her brother pounded on her bedroom door.

"Back the fuck down." Her face heated. "Sorry."

Running Wolf wanted to kill her brother, but he did understand the need to protect the woman under him. He jumped off the bed, adjusting his hard cock in his pants before helping Kizzy up off the bed.

Her cute red cheeks only made him groan at how the pinkness had spread down her neck to the top of her full breasts. "I don't suppose your brother would allow me to help you in the shower?"

"No, he would not," came the response through the door.

Kizzy rested her head against his chest. "I'm afraid until we make it legal, my brother will make an ass out of himself."

"Damn right. You're lucky he's even in the same room with your right now. Just think what Papa would be doing to him now."

"There is need to make your sister ashamed," Running Wolf snapped. "You know damn well she will be my wife." He started toward the door, but she placed her hand on his arm.

"He's just speaking the truth. Don't you think you should ask me before you start telling people we are getting married?" She patted his chest.

Running Wolf grasped her hand, holding her in place. "You will marry me, Little Gypsy, because we were meant to be, but if you need the words...." Dropping to his knees, he rested his head against her bare belly.

"I promise that your life will come before mine. There might be tough times ahead, but my love for you is deep and soul reaching. I might be possessive, demanding, but you, Little Gypsy will stand beside me in this mess that comes our way. I will hold you when you need to cry. I will watch you dance at night under the stars and know that my woman is special. Be mine, Little Gypsy, and let me love you through the tough days ahead of us and to eternity."

"That was beautiful, but it wasn't a question." Kizzy traced his cheek. "Even I know I was meant to be by your side, and where you will be possessive, I will make sure your life is filled with light even when the dark times move in on us. You will be the music I dance to because I already hear the rhythm in my soul." She leaned down to kiss the top of his head, but he stood and covered her mouth with his.

She tried to move away, but he held her tight. "My Gypsy," he whispered against her lips.

"Yours, but don't do that again till I brush my teeth. Yuck." She ducked out of his arms, grabbed her robe from the door, and hurried to fling the door open before he could catch her.

"Damn it, Kizzy. You'll hurt yourself again." Running Wolf went to step into the bathroom, but she closed the door and he heard water running.

"I'm fine, and I'll be out in a few minutes," she yelled.

"So I guess congrats are in order?" Mason slapped his back. "You are in luck. My uncle Santana is ordained and can perform the ceremony." Mason dragged Running Wolf into the living room where his uncles all waited.

"Welcome to the family, son. We should have the wedding before we pack up and leave this place, but not out there where there are so many negative vibes streaming in the air," Stephan said.

"I'm afraid the wedding will have to wait till we dispose of this other threat to her and her friends. I won't have her special day ruined by another shooting," Running Wolf said.

Sun Bull leaned inside. "We need to speak."

"Excuse me, gentlemen." Running Wolf headed toward the door but paused when Stephan and the others got up. "And you are following me because?"

"Because this threat is to our niece, so get used to the idea of us there right next to you until it's over," Santana stated.

"But this might be club business, and I really don't need your help there. It's been a long time since I've had a babysitter." As he stepped onto the porch, his gorge rose at the stench greeting him. "What the hell is that?"

"You need to see this, but I'd put on shoes because you don't even want to step close to this toxic mess," Dark Horse said. "It's the reason for all the threats."

"I'd also be telling your little lady to start tying everything down, because we need to get her and her trailer out of the area. The feds are coming in and the EPA already has men here. It's not safe to stay," Sun Bull explained. "We have three men helping Lone Star and Rose get ready to go as well. I've even sent a trailer in for what can't fit into their trucks."

At that moment, Lone Star drove into the yard and leapt out of his truck. "Where do you want us to go? The other three families are all packing up, as well."

"We will be making a trip to Texas, first. Why don't you and the other families head for Canada and scope out the area, but don't let onto anyone what is going on. I'll have a few of my men meet you there. I'm sorry. I know how hard you and your family worked to make this your home." Running Wolf shook his hand.

"It's not your fault. It's the greed and corruption running wild across these lands. I can honestly understand why the Great Mother is bringing down her judgment on so many."

"My god. What the hell is that stench?" Kizzy asked, stepping outside.

Running Wolf moved her back into the house. "I need you to start getting everything ready so we can move your trailer to a safer location." He cupped her cheek. "I'm sorry, but we have found out what your mayor and the banker have been up to."

"Are Rose and Lone Star okay?" How like her to be concerned for her friends before herself.

"He's just about to head back to finish getting their things packed up. They and the other families will meet us up in Canada after our trip to Texas. They can scout the area so when we do show up, we'll have a better idea of what we are dealing with. One of my men will take care of your home moving there. So if you can pack a small bag to bring with you?" He watched her carefully. Everything was moving so fast.

Instead of arguing, like almost anyone would do in such circumstances, she walked stiffly into her bedroom and knelt beside the bed, pulling out two suitcases, a backpack, and a large carry-on bag. "How small?"

"Let me help you with those." He reached down and lifted her to her feet. "Pack all four of them. You can put the backpack on the bike, and Sun Bull will put the rest in van accompanying us." He placed the bags on the bed. "You can pack them, but do not lift them. We don't need you tearing anything open."

"That's why I'm here." Red Hawk came in. "I'd like to check the wound before she does anything."

"Good and thank you." Running Wolf stepped aside.

"I really am better," Kizzy said.

"Let me judge this, okay?"

She agreed, knowing there was no sense in arguing. Kizzy lowered the peasant blouse down enough Red Hawk could check the wounds.

He prodded the puffy area where he'd removed one bullet. "It's a little red. Did you bump it?"

"I don't think so." Kizzy whimpered.

"Easy there, almost done." He held his palm over the wound until sweat broke out on his forehead. "She'll be okay, but still no lifting anything." Red Hawk turned to face Running Wolf. "I'd like to go with you to Texas. You're going to need me."

"Get ready. I'll be out in a second. I'll need to speak with Frank and Tack before we leave." As the healer went out the door, Running Wolf placed a kiss on her wound. "If he hadn't been healing you, I would have killed him for touching you." He reached up and cupped her cheek. "Never mistake my easygoing nature, Kizzy. I'm a very jealous man, and I'll skin and stake any man who touches what is mine." Grabbing his boots, he headed for the door.

"Running Wolf, what about the mayor and—"

"There is no need to worry. I'm sure they are both on the run or have been caught, but I will find out Tack knows. Stay inside, Little Gypsy." Something major was going to happen, and he wanted Kizzy far, far away from this place before it did.

Chapter Nine

"The rain on my face reminds me of the tears of the souls that walked this world before. Do we add more?" Running Wolf, President White Buffalo MC

Reaching for the third bag to pack, Kizzy found herself staring at the mayor. He stood in the doorway, sweat covering his face, his hair pasted to his head. "Going somewhere, bitch?"

"How did you get in here?" She stumbled back, coming up against her bed.

"With all that is going on, you would think your man would have left someone here to protect you, but his loss. You've cost me too much. I had hoped to set you up in town, but now I'm just going to fuck you and rip out your tongue."

She spun to the right in time to avoid his lunge, leaving him to flop on the mattress.

"Running Wolf! Help!"

She ran to the door only to run into Teter blocking the exit. His fist connected with her cheek, sending her flying back into Dana who grabbed onto her breasts and squeezed them tight.

"We're both going to fuck you." He bit the side of her neck, and she screamed, slamming her head into his nose. Bones crunched, and he shoved her away from him, screaming and grabbing his nose.

She lost her footing and fell forward, right into Teter, who grinned and shoved a knife into her lower stomach. The exact same knife Kizzy had seen in her dream was now sticking out of her. Blood and pain seemed to cover every part of her body and soul.

Her dream was coming true, and there was nothing she could do about it. She fell to her knees then forward, embedding the knife deeper into her.

She sobbed in pain. "Running Wolf, so, so sorry."

Images of Momma, Papa and Mason singing around the fire filled her mind along with her momma's *You have a long life to live, my princess.*

Running Wolf's war cry split the air, and everything went black.

***

Running Wolf had been gone for only twenty minutes when he realized something was wrong and spun around, running back toward his woman. Snatching the knife he wore at his waist, he called for Red Hawk and Dark Horse to follow him.

When she screamed his name, his blood boiled, and he knew he had failed her. Dark Horse beat him to the door and tackled the mayor. Teter was on top of Kizzy, her shirt torn open, blood streaming from her belly. He was yanking at her panties when he glanced up into his eyes.

"You die tonight," Running Wolf cried out and lunged for the man, who yanked the knife out of his woman and tried to stab him with it. Two seconds later, he flung the soon-to-be-dead man out the door. "Red Hawk!"

The healer knelt down next to her lifeless body. Dark Horse threw the mayor out to join his partner in crime.

Blood was everywhere, hers. A bruise started to form on her delicate cheek. "Don't leave me, Little Gypsy. I need you." He placed a kiss on her forehead.

"I will save her," Red Hawk said. "Go and take care of the trash. We'll be here when you are done. I won't fail you, my friend. I was meant to do this." His friend placed his hand over her wound and closed his eyes, employing the healing abilities gifted him by the Great Mother.

Running Wolf placed kiss on her lips and stood slowly, making his way outside where the two men waited for their sentence.

Hate and anger radiated from Stephan. "Do it."

Running Wolf understood. "Tie them up and gag them. They will be returned to the Mother by the means of the toxic waste they have dumped here. Dark Horse, have Tack move some of his men away from part of the pit. Do not tell him why. The less he knows, the better, but he'll listen. Also, let him and Frank know I would speak with them tomorrow at the campground outside of town." He glanced over his shoulder at where Red Hawk attended his woman inside the trailer. "Sun Bull, stay with them."

His friend grasped his shoulder. "I won't leave their side until you are back. I still think you should skin them alive, like the old days."

"They will suffer that fate, but not at our hands. The toxic crap they have dumped into the Earth will not only rip them apart, it will leave nothing for anyone to find."

"You can't do this. You have to give us to the local authorities. Someone help!" Teter yelled, but two of the men stuffed a dirty rag into his mouth and stripped him of his clothes, tying him up like a calf at branding time. His whipped around to the mayor, who hadn't said a word. "You don't beg?"

Dark Horse had already done a number on the man, his fingers broke and his nose bleeding.

"Why? I know where this is going and knew it would happen, but you won't win. No one will survive."

"That is where you are wrong. Those of a true heart will survive. We will build a new world where we will honor the Earth we walk upon and each other." Running Wolf stepped back, and his men gagged and tied the mayor. The Great Mother would take care of these two who had tried to destroy what was hers.

He led the way as his men carried their enemy toward their destination. Dark Horse pointed to where a small fissure had opened and the toxic mess bubbled up.

"May your trip back to the Great Mother be as painful as what you have done to her and my woman." Running Wolf nodded as Teter was dumped first into the hole. The pain and horror in his eyes as the evil doer sank into the liquid mess eased the pain in his heart. He raised his hand and the mayor was thrown into the same hole.

"I've wasted enough time here. I want everyone packed up and ready to roll as soon as I know it's safe to move Kizzy. We'll camp at the place we noted earlier. Once we wrap this mess up with the town, we head for Texas. Dark Horse, call in the rest of the men and have them meet us in Louisville. Make sure they come prepared. Let them know we will be facing the Irons. It seems we are bound to clash one last time."

His men growled and went about their work as he moved toward his woman and her family.

"You are taking Kizzy with you?" Stephan asked.

"Yes, she has already had the vision, and she was there. I have a feeling Dark Horse's woman will need her." He stopped, his attention on her uncle Stephan. "Kizzy died earlier. It's how I knew something was wrong." Running Wolf tipped his head back, staring at the dark skies. "When we were all drawn to Soaring Eagle so long ago, we were told that we would find our chosen one, and when we did, she would perish before our eyes. I truly believe it's a way for our Great Mother to show us soon we all will be grieving for what is about to come. The day of cell phones and computers is slowly coming to end. She does not want us destroyed, or what she's created for us. We all must now listen to her signs."

"You have come a long way, and she approves," Soaring Eagle said. "Your woman is awake and asking for you." He looked around. "All of you. It seems she has seen her mother and father."

Running Wolf almost flew to her little home on wheels. She lay on the couch. Red Hawk was spread out on the floor beside her, his hand still on her latest wound. But her head moved slowly, and Kizzy smiled. "Momma and Papa have given us their blessing."

Red Hawk grunted. "Sun Bull, help me up and take me to wherever we are camping because I'm going sleep a good ten hours." His red tired eyes met his. "She will live, but do not move her right now. I will have to do another healing session with her when I awake, but for now, she needs sleep." Red Hawk patted her shoulder. "Do not overdo it. You tell them what you have to and then sleep. If we are moving this place, she has to be inside it, so I'd suggest making sure everything around her is strapped down."

Running Wolf placed his hand on Red Hawk's arm and squeezed. "Thank you."

"There is no need to thank me. You go out of your way to help us, and we help you. I'll see you in the morning, but, Running Wolf, she won't be able to ride for a few days. So I suggest you have your wedding before we head for Texas."

"It will be done. Now go rest." He moved to sit next to her on the floor, kissing her bruised cheek. "My Little Gypsy, I lost you and was never so afraid in my life."

She traced his cheek with her fingers. "It was good to visit Momma and Papa. They know what is coming and that I would be safe with you."

She beckoned her uncles over. "Ares, Papa told me to tell you to stop blaming yourself. In a way, you saved us all. This path led us to Running Wolf and his group. Our family will be entwined with his. He also said not to worry. You will find the right woman before the darkness comes."

Ares snorted and bent to kiss her cheek. "I need to gather the children and get ready for the move. I love you, little Kizzy. You rest and listen to your man. Soon, you will have that wedding."

Next, Stephan knelt next to her.

A tear rolled down her cheek. "Papa misses you, your games and the tricks you played on each other. He said to protect your back, something about a past enemy not being finished with you."

He also placed a kiss on her cheek. "I, too, miss our games and tricks, but I have your father in my heart, and I'll be careful. Now, rest." He stood, but Kizzy grabbed his leg.

"I was wondering if you would give me away at our wedding. Father wants you standing in his place as the next eldest son."

Stephan snorted. "I'd be honored," He faced Running Wolf. "Treat her well." He rose and left as her last uncle knelt down next to her.

"I feel like some queen with all of you kneeling," She placed her hand on her uncle's cheek. "Dad is worried about you the most. He knows how much you miss Ella. She is there in the next world, Santana. She wants you to move on, to find a woman to raise your daughter." Kizzy scrunched up her face.

"Are you hurting? Do I need to get Red Hawk back here?" Running Wolf asked.

"No, I'm fine, trying to remember. Oh, yeah. The sea is never ending as my love for you. The stars shine bright and my love will always be there...."

"Guiding me," her uncle finished. "I had forgotten her promise and mine. Thank you, little Kizzy." He stood. "I have my truck here, so we can hook this up to it and take it to the campground. I'm already set up there, as are my brothers. Mason, help Running Wolf tie everything down while I get the truck and, you, rest." He tucked a blanket around her.

"You're staying in here with her?" he asked.

"Of course. Dark Horse and Sun Bull will take my bike to the campground. I have most of my belongings here."

"How come I didn't notice them?" Kizzy asked.

He lifted the lid of the coffee table and pulled his backpack from the storage area inside. "I travel light."

She snorted, staring at her brother. "Momma and Papa are proud of you and miss you very much." She swallowed, and tears filled her eyes. "I can have Momma's box now." The air around them grew cold, and she sighed. "Fine, I don't know why no one wants me to have it. I should get something of hers." Kizzy rubbed her arms.

"That I can help with, but not now." Mason leaned down, nose to nose with her. "You were not meant to deal with curses and killing. Your heart is too pure. Let us handle the other stuff. You just do your thing with you were born with." He kissed her nose and moved to the bedroom. "I'll start locking stuff down. I take it the house is going north when we head for Texas?"

Running Wolf stood. "Yes, I want her home safe in Canada when we face the Irons. I wish you could go, but I have a feeling you are going to be needed with Dark Horse's woman."

"She's been hurt emotionally, and I'm afraid these Irons, whoever they are, are the ones doing it, but it's not new. They've been there for a bit." Kizzy's eyes widened. "They know you are coming. They've been preparing for this."

"Stop worrying, I already kind of figured that. I've called in everyone. They'll meet us in Louisville." Running Wolf kissed her lips and stood again, attaching the straps to the doors so they stayed shut.

"How big is your motorcycle club?" she asked.

"You'll see." He pointed at the rug. "I'm afraid this has to go, Kizzy. It's ruined." She trembled. "Hey now, it's all over. They can't touch you again. Both of them are back with the Great Mother." Running Wolf said.

Her brother rolled up the rug and tossed it out the door. "I'll start working on the floor." He moved to the kitchen. "The bedroom is all locked down."

"Use the blue bottle. It will get out the blood. Someone should make sure the bathroom shelves are closed up, too, please," Kizzy said.

"I'm here, Little Gypsy," Running Wolf said. "Close your eyes and relax, knowing I'm right here."

"You won't leave?"

"No, never again will you be unprotected I promise. I failed you once, but not again." She would be guarded at all times even if she didn't like it.

Chapter Ten

"The sun is shining for today, but I heard the story of the Dark Days coming. Are you ready? Are you prepared?" Dark Horse, White Buffalo MC

Kizzy took a deep breath, staring at her new surroundings. They had been at the campsite now for two days, and it was the first time she had been out of bed. It not only had been hell sleeping next to Running Wolf not being able to start anything, but having her uncles there as chaperones was a total pain. But, tonight, she and Running Wolf would be married.

Already Running Wolf had been run out of her little house and threatened with mayhem by Uncle Stephan if he got too close to her until the ceremony. He had grumbled and kissed her hard, but he had removed himself, leaving Dark Horse there to protect her.

"I know you are there watching me, so come, take a walk with me. We have some things to discuss." She waited for said warrior to let his presence be known.

He moved at his own pace, slowly scanning everything around him, a lopsided smile on his face. "You are going to give the boss a run for his money. Are you sure you are up to going for a walk?"

"Red said I could for a little while, plus I need to tell you a bit about your woman." She tucked her arm into his when he stiffened. "Relax you need to know this because, Dark Horse, I know all about your loving ways. Running Wolf tried to explain a few things. It was kind of cute."

Dark Horse snorted and led her toward a path in the forest. "Only you would call our fearless leader cute. Tell me about my woman, please."

"I have a feeling she has grown up around these Iron Horse people and is kind of prisoner there. She has tried to leave, but they always block her path. She's never known the world, only the small part they have allowed her to explore." Kizzy stopped, staring up at him. "I know our times are growing short here, but after all this stuff with the Irons is done, if you could just take her someplace magical for her to remember, before the shit hits the fan." Kizzy started to walk again. "I've always wanted to visit Europe, but I know we don't have time for that. Wait. I know. Take her to the Smokey Mountains." She jumped up and moaned.

"Damn it, Kizzy, don't go and hurt yourself. I'll never hear the end of it from Running Wolf."

"I'm fine, just shouldn't have jumped yet. Anyway, something like the Smokey Mountains or even Vegas would be great. She could witness both aspects of the world, one where everyone is pampered and one where nature takes your breath away."

Dark Horse stepped in front of her. "Was she raped?"

"You know the answer to that." She shivered. "For the last six years, they have emotionally and physically abused her. She'll need a gentle hand, but once Lilly opens up, she'll be the one you need. It's going to take a while for her to trust any of us fully, but you hold the key to her."

"What? I don't even know her. How can I hold the key?" He looked at her like she'd lost her mind.

She patted his arm. "Come on. Take me to the pond. I want to see how the decorations are going for tonight." Once more, they started to walk. "As for how you will be the key, she's a slave at heart, Dark Horse. Lilly needs a gentle hand, but someone to take control."

He grinned. "Like Running Wolf does with you?"

"We haven't even broached that, yet. Stephan walked in while Running Wolf was trying to explain a few things. But, in my case, not as much as Lilly. Of course I want Running Wolf's guidance, and I know he will protect me, but I also know I can dress myself and do things to keep busy. Your Lilly is going to need you to build her up from the ground. She is nothing but their whipping dog, Dark Horse."

They stepped into the clearing.

"I'll kill every one of them, I swear," Dark Horse said, earning glances from Sun Bull and Night Song.

"Who are you going to kill?" Uncle Stephan asked, joining them.

"We were talking about the Irons and his woman. So, are we all set? Did we find my flowers?" she asked.

"All is just like you wanted it. But don't you think you should be resting, especially if you plan to have an evening like all couples enjoy on their wedding night?" Stephan said.

Her face heated. "You didn't need to bring that up, and I'm fine. Red Hawk will stop by this afternoon and check in on me before the wedding. Now, where is my soon-to-be husband?"

Stephan placed a kiss on her head. "He and a few of his men rode into town to clean up the mess and speak with friends."

"But, is it safe? You know Teter and the mayor were not the only ones. What about the sheriff and his men?" Her attention went back to Dark Horse. "I don't like this."

"Relax. If anything, the idiots that are left had better not let Running Wolf find them. Plus, he took some of our best fighters with him, so he'll be good."

For the next hour, Kizzy roamed around the area, pointing out things she wanted changed, wishing her mom was there with her.

"Kizzy I have something for you." Mason approached, carrying a box she had never seen. "Come over here and sit. You don't need to lift anything yet." Mason settled her at the picnic table and placed the large box in front of her, lifting the lid. "Momma did think of you. She gave this to me about a year before they were killed and made me promise to give it to you on your wedding day."

Her hands shook as Kizzy traced her finger over the antique white gown her mother had worn at her own wedding. Tears rolled down her cheeks. "Momma's dress?"

"You know what hell it's going to start when you come walking out in that?" Mason teased her. "I can still hear Papa grumbling and glaring at Momma when he told the story."

Stephan laughed. "But your momma was one of the most beautiful brides. In some ways, Kizzy takes after her momma, connected to the Earth around us. So we'll have a few black eyes, but Running Wolf will never forget his wedding date, will he?" They all laughed, some of the tension slipping from her body.

"That is true. Every May twentieth, Papa would sweep Momma up and take her away for the night, and I have a feeling your warrior is going to be the same way with you, little sister." Mason turned his head to the east where the sound of bikes could be heard. "I'd better tell him to stay back till we get you inside. There is more under the dress, but you need to go now."

Stephan grabbed the box and helped her stand. "I can take the box if you have things to do?" Dark Horse offered.

"No, I'll spend today helping my niece get ready for her big day, but my wife will be arriving along with the rest of our family, so please make sure your men know to expect them." Stephan wrapped his arm around her and walked her toward her home, but stopped, staring back at Dark Horse. "There are close to sixty more men and women coming."

At Dark Horses expression Stephan said. "When I said family I meant it. Cousins, uncles, aunts, we all travel together. The women and the children will follow behind us in case of trouble. They will also be going north when we leave here." Her uncle looked at her. "As I wish you were going."

"Nope, I'm going to be needed, and I won't let Dark Horse or any other of Running Wolf's men down. Come on. I want to explore what else my momma left me." Kizzy started up the path as Running Wolf and his men stepped into the clearing on the other side.

Stephan slipped in front of her, blocking her view of him. "Damn it, Uncle Stephan."

"You will be with him tonight."

Dark Horse snorted. "Not to worry. Running Wolf is cussing up a storm as your other uncle is holding him back."

"That is not funny," she grumbled.

Running growled as Santana held him back. "You can't see her till tonight, but she is fine. It's time to get you ready anyway."

"I picked up a suit," Running Wolf said, but her uncle was shaking his head.

"Nope, we have the formal wear of our people. Like Kizzy will be wearing her mother's dress, you will wear her father's. We are lucky my aunt was here earlier and is waiting to fit the clothes. Now come."

"Really? You have formal wear?" Running Wolf would do anything for his Little Gypsy.

"Believe me, you have little to worry about till you get a glance at Kizzy in her momma's dress," her uncle grumbled.

"What's wrong with her momma's dress?" Running Wolf asked.

Santana flipped back the tent flap. "I'll tell you about my brother's wedding while you are getting fitted, but be warned, it's already been written and you cannot change what is going to happen. It means much that Kizzy wears her mother's dress, so you will not object, understood?"

"Why do I get the feeling I'm doomed here?"

The old woman grinned up at him. "It won't be so bad. Our Kizzy will be a vision just like her momma. But Kizzy is closer to the Earth than her mother was, so remember that when you get your first glance of her. Part of her dress will be formed by the Great Mother herself."

He frowned when she handed him a pair of silky black pants.

"If you are a bashful one, you can go behind that screen and change."

"No, I'm fine." He slipped off his jeans then pulled on the pants right there. He found a hidden pocket.

"We might enjoy the night, but we are not stupid. We protect what is ours," Santana said.

"I knew you were about the same size as our lost soul. Even the length is perfect. I bet the shirt fits also." She pinned and tucked and shooed him away with the promise that in thirty minutes his clothes would be ready for him.

"The pig has been cooking all night. There will be food in abundance for your wedding feast," Santana said. "This is what family is about. Each person in our group will protect you with their life."

"You honor me, and I promise you Kizzy will be protected at all costs," Running Wolf replied.

"Running Wolf," Soaring Wolf called.

"Is something wrong?"

"This town does not have much time left. The Great Mother is holding off, but she wants to claim this land once more and those remaining here will not survive," Soaring Eagle announced.

"Do we warn the town?"

"It will do no good. They are already angry at being betrayed. I sent Penn and Night Song into town. They will inform a few who have helped us. Perhaps others will listen as well."

Chapter Eleven

"Enjoy what you can. Do not dwell in what is yet to come. Each day is given to us as a gift. Don't waste it." Kizzy, Running Wolf's woman.

Kizzy stared at herself in the full-length mirror her uncle Stephan had brought into the small tent outside the clearing. Her three cousins stood behind her, grinning from ear to ear at their handiwork. Curled ringlets twined with baby's breath fell down her back. The silky dress hugged her, leaving hardly anything covered.

"Wow," she whispered, seeing even the outline of her nipples and part of her hair at the junction between her legs. Even more were the live red flowers positioned in certain spots covering, but giving glimpses of her body.

"Your mother's flowers were a lilac color, but red suits you, Little Kizzy," her Uncle Stephan said. "You are absolutely stunning. I have something for you." He pulled out a jewelry box and opened it. "This was your great-grandmothers." He knelt and patted his thigh. "Put your foot up here." Her uncle fastened the diamond-and-ruby anklet.

"It's beautiful, but don't you think one of your daughters should have it?"

"Kizzy, this is your legacy. Your father gave it to me last year to hold onto for you." He sighed. "I have a feeling both of your parents knew something was going to happen. They just didn't know when." He stood and kissed her forehead. "You are marrying a good man."

"Please tell me you didn't do the background thing?"

"Of course, but not to worry. He is clean as a whistle, but we also know your parents approve of him, as does the Great Mother it seems." He touched one of the red flowers on her dress. "It's amazing what the Great Mother can do."

He stepped back, and her brother slid five bracelets up her bare arm. "You can borrow these today. They were Momma's. She gave them to Rona when we got married. So now you have something new, borrowed and..." Mason stepped back to reveal Dark Horse holding a blue garter belt.

Her cheeks heated. "Dark Horse?"

"Running Wolf is like a brother to me, and you've gone out of your way to help me. I would give you this." He scanned her from head to toe. "I think I'll let you put this on. I do believe Running Wolf would have my head if I did it." He handed her the new garter.

"Thank you." She stepped forward and placed a kiss on his cheek. "We both will miss you, but I expect you to keep us informed on how things are going after we leave." She peeked over her shoulder. "But when things settle, we will see each other again." Kizzy pointed to the ground where a single daffodil had sprouted. "Do you know what they say about the daffodil?" She bent down and picked the flower. "It supposed to mark new beginnings, and I believe we are all going to have them." Kizzy placed the flower in his dress shirt buttonhole. "Even you, Dark Horse."

A single tear rolled down his cheek. "My mother always planted these all around our trailer when I was young. I once asked her why just those flowers." He looked up at her. "She said, 'Because, one, in the future you will begin anew. I won't be with you physically, but I will be in your heart. Two, every time you see one of these beautiful flowers, remember I love you and know you are born to lead.' My mother was killed two weeks later."

"The Great Mother knows this and sent you a sign. I know how important you are to Running Wolf. We had a nice talk the other night about a few of you. Your momma would be proud of you." Kizzy reached up and squeezed his arm. "Now go while I put this on because if I'm not mistaken, it's time."

Stephen lifted the tent flap, checking the sky like old times. "Yes it is, the sun is setting."

Dark Horse stopped just outside the flap. "I will always be there for you, Little Kizzy. I pledge my protection to you as long as I'm around."

"And I pledge my protection to you, too," she said, earning a laugh from all of them. "What? I can hurt someone if I have to." She glared at her uncle and brother who were shaking their heads.

"Only you, Little Kizzy." Stephan slapped Dark Horse on the shoulder. "Tell them we'll be ready in about two minutes."

Kizzy trembled inside and out as she bent and put on the garter Dark Horse had given her. She was really going to marry a man she'd met only four days ago. But Running Wolf had shared many personal things as she was healing. He, too, had lost his parents, and Soaring Eagle was more of a father figure than his ever was.

Alcohol had dealt a heavy hand to his father, leaving his mother alone with an eight-year-old boy to raise. Kizzy took a deep breath, refusing to allow the tears to come, even though they had flowed freely at the time he had told her. He had explained many on the reservations had given up, suicide and drinking were rampant, but never once had Running Wolf touched a drink after what it had done to his father.

She stood and adjusted the dress. She had on barefoot sandals her great aunt had made for her, one of the customs of her people to have their feet touching the Great Mother while asking her for her blessing. The groom would wear no shoes or socks, despite their formal attire, from white pearls and green twine. Kizzy couldn't stand to wear shoes, and their custom was to have nothing between.

"You ready?" Stephan moved to her side.

"Yes, just a little nervous." Her cousins ran around and fixed the train of her dress as they walked out of the tent. Stephan and Mason both would give her away. Stephan felt it was only right her older brother participate in that role.

Cousin Benny strummed the guitar, and all eyes focused on her as she made her way down the path to the bonfire. Gasps erupted from Running Wolf's group, but her family only smiled. What had her grinning like a fool was her future husband's growl upon seeing her.

He was going to kill her uncle. "That isn't a dress. It's a peep show." Running Wolf elbowed Dark Horse who snickered. "And every single one of the men is getting a nice free show."

Whistles and howls rolled over the music, but she was a goddess, with her long hair and peeks of what was about to be his enticing him and everyone around them.

"Just think. You have to stay around for the party afterward, too. Everyone gets to dance with her," Dark Horse teased him.

Stephan placed her hand into Running Wolf's and twined some

gold-colored string around their joined hands. "Today, we do not lose a niece, sister, cousin. Instead, we gain another warrior, a nephew, brother, cousin. I give you our Little Kizzy, knowing you are and will put her welfare above your own." Stephan kissed Kizzy's cheek as her brother smiled at her.

"Our parents would be proud, knowing you have kept true to yourself, helping those who need it, but now you have someone that will join you in your mission in life, saving others. I believe you each will save the other and keep each other balanced." Mason looked at him. "Hurt her, and I'll learn how to skin a person."

"Understood," Running Wolf said.

"Our ceremony is simple." Santana knelt and placed his hands into the soil. "Great Goddess, we stand before you, another couple asking for your acceptance so they may walk the rest of their lives together, bound by love and honor." Santana bowed his head, as did Kizzy and her family, so Running Wolf followed suit, giving her family the respect it deserved. What he wasn't expecting was the small green vines wrapping around his legs and hers.

The vines inched up their bodies, flowers blooming on them. Shouts of praise rose to the goddess as Santana stood. "It is done. You two are now joined, not only by a piece of paper, but by the approval of the great goddess herself. In times of hardship, there will be signs of hope and your joining is one. May your lives be rich and full, your children plentiful, and may the goddess keep you both safe. You may kiss your bride, if you can get to her."

"What? What about our vows?" Running Wolf asked.

"There is no need for vows. If you were not true to your heart, the Great Mother would not have approved." Santana glanced at his brother, Ares.

"As Soaring Eagle has been close to the Great Mother, we have always asked for her acceptance when we marry, and some of us listen, while some of us don't. You have been honored, but you must earn that first kiss as a husband and wife," Ares stated. "You must free yourselves of the vines."

The vines were tight. Running Wolf could break them, but he had to be careful not to hurt his wife. It took him a good five minutes to finally figure out how to slide the vines off both of them, taking his prize, his wife.

Shouts broke out, and the music started again, but Running Wolf had to admit he loved his woman tied up, waiting for him. Kizzy tasted of berries as he covered her mouth, sliding his tongue in, exploring. He couldn't get enough, but everyone waited for them.

He broke the kiss, resting his forehead against hers. "I have something for you." Running Wolf put out his hand for the ring "This was my mother's ring, and now it's yours." He slid the ring on her wedding finger. "It's not much, but it's old and the inscription says forever. You are mine forever, my Little Gypsy."

"It's stunning and perfect. I have something for you." She handed him a box. "I asked Soaring Eagle, and he helped me with this. If you don't like it, you don't have to wear it."

Inside the box lay a small leather pouch.

"Soaring Eagle told me you didn't have one, now you can make it yours. I added a part of me inside it." She lifted a strand of her hair. "And I gathered all the herbs Soaring Eagle told me about, so all you have to do now is personalize it for you."

Never had anyone done anything for him like this, except for his mother and Soaring Eagle. Soaring Eagle's helping her also made it special. "You are a gift that I will treasure always, my Little Gypsy. It's beyond amazing, thank you." He leaned over and kissed her lips softly. "Tonight, my wife."

Chapter Twelve

"Tradition and new come together to create a new family, bound by the souls of two people." Kizzy, Running Wolf's Wife

The torches around the campsite lit the path Kizzy walked, needing to get away from all the music and hugs. She had done it, gotten married, but with a future so unreal it had her shaking when she thought of what was to come.

Already, Kizzy could notice the changes in the forest. Animals were scarce, and it wasn't peaceful like it had been growing up as a child. Taking walks at night and listening to everything around her had been a habit, a need of hers to calm and soothe her, but now only the stars were the same.

She stepped over a fallen tree and carefully sat down on it, staring up at the night sky. Running Wolf was giving his men orders for breaking up camp tomorrow. They would head for Texas and the big battle that she knew was coming.

But tonight would be her first night with Running Wolf. Oh, she wasn't a virgin, but the last time Kizzy had been with a man or boy, he had taken her virginity a long time ago, at least it seemed. Would she be up to Running Wolf's standards? Could she keep him happy? She ran her hand over the little scar that had formed on her stomach. Kizzy still couldn't believe she had died that night.

If she didn't know better, Kizzy would think her life was turning into one of those romances she liked to read every so often. Once they were at their final destination, a library of some kind would be set up, since it was obvious they would be without Internet and such for a while.

A branch snapped behind her, and she jumped. Running Wolf

stood there with his arms crossed over his chest.

"I leave for a few seconds, and you take off. Do you know how dangerous it is for you to be out here alone?" He gave her a look that sent a shiver down her spine.

"Sorry. I always take a walk at night to calm down before I go to bed." Kizzy patted the spot next to her. "Is it me, or does the night sound off. Like even the animals have started to leave this area?"

"You are right. Soaring Eagle mentioned to me that the city will be given back to the Mother soon." Running Wolf sat down beside her and lifted her into his lap. "Little Gypsy, with the dangerous times moving in on us, you can't go wandering by yourself. Now promise me if you want to take a walk, you'll seek me out." He placed a kiss on her neck.

She rested her head against his chest. "I promise. I was thinking there is so much to do before all this happens. We need seeds for planting. I'd like to start collecting books so the children and adults will have material to help the time pass as we are held up in our areas, not to mention we need food staples."

"Relax. Tonight is for us. Tomorrow will come soon enough. Now, about this dress, my Little Gypsy…"

"I've seen bathing suits expose more than I did. You didn't like it?"

"I love it, but that is the kind of dress you wear for just me only." He nipped her shoulder. "And don't even think any of our daughters will wear it."

"Of course, our daughter would wear her mother's, and grandmother's dress. It is a tradition." She laughed and placed a kiss on his chest. "What time do we leave tomorrow?"

Running Wolf held her in his arms. "Early. That's why we are on our own now. I have a special place all set up for us so we can be alone." He moved them deeper into the woods until she could hear running water. "I was told about this part of the park earlier, and it's not been affected by the crap they dumped."

They emerged into a scene from one of her books. Torches lit a tent. In the background a waterfall spilled into a small lake. A round table with two chairs sat in front of the tent.

"The lady at the bakery in town heard about our wedding and was determined you have a cake even if it was a small one." Running Wolf placed his hand on her back as she moved toward the table holding a personal-sized cake topped with red and purple flowers. "Lisa, I think her name was, said the cake was German chocolate.

She seemed to think that was your favorite."

Kizzy sat down, shaking her head. "You didn't have to do all this. We could have used my home."

He joined her and took her hand. "My Little Gypsy, you deserve so much more than this. I would give you the world if I could. Our life will not be easy, and I will be possessive and demanding of you, but you will always know I love you." He cut two small pieces of cake. "I do believe we are supposed to feed each other?"

Before she could even turn toward him, Running Wolf reached down her dress and pulled her breast out smashing the cake all over it. "Now I'll eat."

"Hey that's not faireee."

"I don't play fair," he said, licking and sucking the cake from her. "And I never will, when it comes to you. We can eat cake after I take what is mine." He sucked on her breast, scooping her up and carrying her inside the tent.

Running Wolf lowered her to her feet then reached for her zipper. He had been waiting a lifetime for this minute, and he was about to take his time making this night special for Kizzy.

He slid the dress down her stunning body, pausing to trace the small scar. "Every time I see this little mark, I'll know how lucky I am to still have you here with me." Careful not to step on her dress, Running Wolf lifted her up and placed her on the silk sheets. Her ringlets spread out around her, and he stared at the stunning beauty before him.

He lay beside her, kissing and touching every inch of her pale, soft skin.

He slowly made his way down her stomach, pausing to place a kiss on his mark, and it was his. His failure to protect her, his proof she had died for him, and her love for him, fighting to stay alive, to be at his side.

Kizzy lifted her head and ran her hand through his hair. "Hey, stop fretting so much."

"I will always cherish you, my Little Gypsy." He scooted down and parted her pussy lips. "Grab your legs and hold yourself open for me." He inhaled her scent then licked her outer lips. "As sweet as that cake."

"You most likely got a piece of the cake on your chin. My god," she whimpered, holding her legs back as he slid his tongue into her.

Her cream covered his lower face. "Please."

Her head tossed back and forth when he slid a finger into her. His Little Gypsy was tight, squeezing his finger. "No cake, just Little Gypsy. Come for me, Kizzy. Let me see your body dance." He sucked her little clit into his mouth, adding another finger inside her.

She released her legs, her back arched, and she grabbed onto the covers, squeezing until her knuckles were white. His Little Gypsy released the breath she was holding, gasping and moaning as she tried to close her legs and move away from him, but he was far from done.

Running Wolf hooked his fingers and found that special rough spot inside her. "Again."

"Running Wolf!" Kizzy's legs trembled against his arms, her wetness placing a tiny love spot on the bed as another orgasm played over her body.

He withdrew, placing a kiss on the inside of her thigh before getting off the bed and stripping out of his shirt.

Kizzy licked her lips, her glazed eyes following his movements as he stripped out of his wedding clothes.

"Do I meet with your approval?" Running Wolf stroked his cock.

"I'd have to be dead not be affected by your body." Kizzy flinched. "Sorry, didn't mean that. You are amazing. How can I have someone so handsome, fierce, and kind in my life?" She met his gaze as he crawled onto the bed over her.

"If you say you don't deserve me, I'm going to spank your butt." He leaned down and nipped her nipple, sliding his cock up and down her pussy lips. Lifting her knees, he opened her and slid slowly inside.

She grabbed his shoulders.

"Damn." He covered her mouth. Every inch of her tasted sweet, her mouth no exception.

Her little moans and whimpers as he started to move in and out of her going, farther in with each movement drove Running Wolf crazy. He broke the kiss. The trust and love in her eyes as she stared up at him humbled him more than anything he could say. "I'll make you happy, my Little Gypsy," he promised before thrusting in and out of her faster, harder.

He wasn't going to last much longer, but she would come with him, squeezing his cock, milking his seed. He paused, the thought of her belly swollen with his baby sent a chill across his damp skin.

Possessiveness and the need to have their child at her breast sent an ache into his chest.

"What's wrong?" Kizzy asked.

"I want a baby." Running Wolf released her legs and began to thrust with new purpose.

She inched her arms up around his neck and pulled him down. "Our child growing in me, well, I would love it. Now, love me, my warrior, like you're riding into battle. You've caught me. Show me what a fine warrior like you can do."

Running Wolf was not one to disappoint his woman. "Hold on tight because this warrior is going to show you how your man loves to ride his woman."

Chapter Thirteen

"Those of a true heart will survive. We will build a new world where we will honor the Earth we walk upon and each other." Running Wolf, President White Buffalo MC

Running Wolf seemed to know Kizzy's every move. Just having him inside her, his hands moving over her skin, mouth sucking on breasts had her toes curling, and, for the first time in a long time, Kizzy felt alive.

He reached down and squeezed her ass cheeks, lifting her hips. His thrusts were hard, quick, hitting the magical spot inside her.

Kizzy dug her nails into his shoulders. "More, please." Her legs trembled, and little beads of sweat formed at her temples and rolled down her neck. "Running Wolf!" she screamed as once more her warrior sent her over to the land of extreme pleasure, but this time he joined her, his seed warm inside her.

"My Little Gypsy!" He pumped once, twice, three more times before rolling over and bringing her on top of him, still connected to him.

"Hmm, I do believe I have been served." Kizzy rubbed her cheek on his chest and kissed him there. "You my warrior are amazing. Do you really want a child now?"

"You don't want one?" He brushed her hair out of her eyes.

"I want lots of children, but don't you think it would be wiser to wait till we get where we are going? Or do you think we will be there soon?"

Running Wolf placed a kiss on her cheek. "I believe we will be in Canada in a couple of months, so I see no problems starting our family now. But, when we get to Texas, you will stay out of the way.

The Irons are not a group to mess with, and I have a feeling we are going to have a bad time with them."

"I can help. I'm not useless. Matter of fact, I'm a perfect shot. Just ask my brother."

"As in guns?"

"Shotgun, handgun." Kizzy shrugged. "Dad would take me out in the woods to practice all the time. He said I would need to learn how to clean and handle all sort of guns. I also know how to shoot a bow and arrow, even though they are usually too big for me."

"I'm surprised. Your brother and uncles don't want you touching any weapons, and I have to agree. You, my Little Gypsy, should not have to worry about protecting yourself or anyone else."

Sadness settled over her. "We are all going to have to know how to defend ourselves. Whatever happens is not going to be pretty, and I'm sorry to say humans react without thinking most of the time. Sometimes it seems animals have more sense than us, you know?"

"Yes, I know. Over the past ten years I have come across some of the worst of our kind, but I don't want you doing anything unless it is to protect yourself. I have a feeling it would cost you more to hurt someone than you are letting on, no?"

"Well, maybe, but if I was threatened or my family or any children, I have no qualms doing what is necessary. Would it bother me? Yes, but I have you to help me out of it." She placed another kiss on his chest and sat up. "Now would be a great time for that cake and maybe some milk?"

Running Wolf rolled her over, pulling out of her. "Let's get some food into you because our night has just begun." He jumped off the bed and held out his hand.

She placed her hand into his, and he pulled her up. Kizzy's legs still shook a little from their lovemaking, and the jerk grinned at her. "How is it I'm still wobbly and our lovemaking has no effect on you?"

He helped her into her robe then wrapped his arms around her. "Remember, I ride a bike and horse all the time. My legs are stronger. Plus, if I don't set you off balance, our lovemaking isn't what it should be." Running Wolf squeezed her bottom cheeks. "Has anyone loved your ass?"

She stiffened and glared up at him. "He tried, but it didn't go well. Running Wolf, I've only been with one man. So I'm afraid if you need experience, I have none, sorry."

He threw on a pair of jeans and swung her up in his arms. "Do not apologize for that. It means more to me that I get to teach you all the different ways we can explore our bodies together. Starting tonight." He carried her outside and set her in one of the chairs. With perfect timing, Mason came out of the woods with a cooler, followed by her uncle Stephan carrying two covered plates. Dark Horse's ice bucket held a frosty bottle.

"Please don't tell me they were sitting out there waiting for us…" Her face grew warm and she wanted to kick Running Wolf.

He threw his head back and laughed. "No, Little Gypsy. I told them to give us a couple of hours." He planted a hard kiss on her lips. "Trust your man. I wouldn't embarrass you on purpose."

"Yes he would, if you were into that kind of loving." Dark Horse earned a punch. "But it's obvious you are not into the degrading thing." He rubbed his arm.

"Ha, anyone try and do that to my sister, she'll get even. Believe me." Mason set the cooler down. "Remember that time I embarrassed you when you were a freshmen and I was a senior?"

"You so, so deserved that, even though I did get in trouble with the school. Dad didn't know if he should laugh or discipline me." Kizzy smiled at Running Wolf. "You know how freshmen are picked on? Well, dipshit here decided to lay it on thick since I was his sister. Not only did he tell everyone about how I had an accident the first time I rode a rollercoaster, he went on to tell everyone that I slept with a light on, which I only did because I had a habit of sleepwalking when I was younger."

Running Wolf raised an eyebrow. "What did she do to you?"

Mason grinned. "The little bugger here not only got me but my best friends, too. We had been playing basketball at lunch, and she snuck into the locker room, stole all our clothes then proceeded to display our underwear in the cafeteria. Back in those days, there was only one gym teacher and she was female," he grumbled. "I still get ribbed about that from the guys when I talk to them."

Everyone laughed as her uncle Stephan placed the two plates of food in front of them. "Eat. I know for a fact you two didn't eat earlier. Oh, and I wanted to let you know we have packed everything up and your little house is on its way north. We packed your laptop and other things you might need in the truck to go to Texas."

"I really don't like you going through my things." She stuffed her mouth with potato salad.

"Why would you have—" Mason scrunched up his face. "Now, that thought was just eww."

Stephan cuffed him on the head. "Knock it off. Each person has a right to whatever they please. If toys please her—"

Kizzy got up and clapped a hand over his mouth. "Enough already, jeez. It's nothing really. We should eat." She placed a kiss on her uncle's cheek. "Thanks for bringing us the food. I'll see you tomorrow." Kizzy patted his chest and her brother's, about to go to Dark Horse when Running Wolf dragged her back against his body.

"I have to thank Dark Horse." She struggled, but he held her tight.

Dark Horse snorted. "He's not going to allow you to touch me right now, Kizzy. As I said, our prez is a very possessive man, as I would be. But I know you meant well. Plus, I got a kiss earlier from you." Dark Horse headed into the woods before Running Wolf could do anything.

"You're lucky I'd rather hold *my* woman than come over there and pound on you," Running Wolf said into her neck, nipping it. "We will discuss what you have in that little home of yours you don't want others to know about while we eat."

***

Running Wolf hid the smile as his wife sputtered and her face pinked a little as she settled into the seat across from him.

"Really, Running Wolf, it's not a big deal." Mason and her Uncle Stephan melted into the woods, but there were other men stationed there, protecting them while he spent the night with his woman.

From now on, their guard would always be on the lookout, not knowing what was going to happen or when. He wasn't about to allow anything to happen to his world, his wife.

"What?" Kizzy took a bite of the roasted pig on her plate.

"Just realizing how much you mean to me. To think, a week ago I had no clue you were going to come into my life, and now, here we are married." He tasted the meat. "Damn, your family can cook."

"Should we have waited?" Doubt played on her face.

Running Wolf rose and moved to her side right away, not liking the doubt on her face. "Little Gypsy." He swung her chair around, and moved between her legs, smelling their combined scent still on her. "We might have had a short courtship, but you were meant to be mine. I don't know how to explain it, but it's like your gift you have soothing people. But once I heard your voice, I knew I had to be with you. When you died, it was like there was a hole in my heart.

Never, never doubt that we were meant to be together." He cupped her cheek. "I was thinking about why now and so quick. With the dark times closing in on us, the Great Mother knew we would need our women standing next to us, helping those who will join us. But never for once think I don't love you, because I do."

She ran a hand through his hair. "You really believe the Great Mother is doing all this? Leading us where she wants us to be? Or some other supreme being is planning something? Do you ever think maybe they're not gods but aliens who helped populate this world and got tired of seeing it destroyed?"

Running Wolf covered her mouth, loving her beyond words. "You, Little Gypsy, are crazy. After our own wedding, do you really believe that?"

"Do I believe that there are others out there? Yes. But as to the Great Mother? I believe she is as real as you and me." Kizzy bit her lip. "Go eat before your food gets cold. I'll tell you something that happened to me when I was fourteen, but if you laugh at me, I'm throwing our cake at you."

"I would never laugh at you, baby." He kissed the top of her head and moved to his seat. "And don't think I forgot about what you have hidden in your home." He took a bite of potato salad. "We will discuss that next."

"My cousin Ella makes the best potato salad and coleslaw." She took a bite, chewed and swallowed. "Anyway, when I was fourteen, my best friend was killed by some nutjob. He had come for me. I had started drawing the creeps the year before, but really thought nothing of it till that day. So this whacko slit her throat in front of me. My uncles, dad, and brother came running before he could get me. For days after Trish was buried, I couldn't sleep. If I tried to eat, I'd get sick. Mom and Dad were flipping out, afraid I'd die because I was losing weight, hair, the whole thing. They finally took me to the hospital. After running all their tests, the doctor gave me something that knocked me out. That's when she visited me."

"Who?" he asked, hearing the hurt and uncertainty in her voice. "Your friend?"

"Trish told me she was, but she was also mad she had to leave so soon and would miss everyone. Then a woman appeared, surrounded by light, but plants grew up around her as she moved forward. Beautiful and so caring, she pulled Trish into her arms, holding her, and stared at me. I can't remember what she looked like, but I can still remember the peace I felt in her presence. She

71

didn't talk. Her thoughts were in my head.

"She told me not to worry, that I had a long journey ahead, and then they vanished and I woke up. It was the next day, fluids had been pumped into me, and they let me go. Mason laughed when I told him about it, so I tackled him. He wasn't expecting it. I had never done anything like that before, but it hurt that he didn't believe me. Anyway, he stumbled and fell backward onto a table, breaking it. Mom and Dad came running into the room. My dad had just fixed that table from when Mason and his friends broke it the week before."

"Did you tell your folks?" Running Wolf asked.

"Yeah." She fed him a bite of her aunt's Waldorf salad. "They thought I dreamed it, but I knew she was real. I was visited again after my parents were killed by the same woman. But even that visit didn't ease the ache. And now we all know it was my fault they were killed." She pushed her food away.

He took her hand. "It is not your fault. It was your aunt's. She was sick in the head, Little Gypsy. I'm afraid we're going to have a lot more of those crazy people to come, especially when things start to get nasty." Running Wolf rose and drew her along with him. "Let's take a dip before we have our dessert."

Chapter Fourteen

"How can this be called work when your heart knows it must be done for others to survive?" Running Wolf, President White Buffalo MC

Kizzy lifted her disposable camera, happy her cousin had given it to her last night and took pictures of her honeymoon suite/forest. How gentle Running Wolf had been making love to her in the water, his love words for her, placing little hickey bites all up and down her neck and shoulders.

They hadn't fallen asleep until at least two in the morning after finishing their cake and the bottle of champagne. She'd tucked the cork in her backpack. Kizzy giggled, remembering the look on Running Wolf's face as she made him search for the cork after he popped it open.

"You want me to what? In the dark?" he had said. But, in about ten minutes, he found it. She'd made sure her husband was truly rewarded for his hard work. She'd dropped to her knees and taken him into her mouth, performing her first blowjob.

Oh sure, many boys had asked, but before Running Wolf, the thought had been gross to her. The camera clicked again as she took another picture of the waterfall. Her sex life was going to be interesting.

"There you are." Running Wolf slid his arms around her and pulled her back against his chest, placing a kiss on her neck. "Weren't you told not to wander off by yourself?"

She slid her hands around his neck, staring up at his handsome face. "I've decided to take all the pictures of things that are beautiful on our ride, starting with our honeymoon night. I want our children to know how precious our world was, at least the parts we didn't destroy. If we get a chance, maybe we can do a before and after." She shrugged. "When we stop for a break, I'd like to buy some more cameras, if that is okay with you?"

He placed his chin on top of her head. "I have no problem with that. I've got the bike packed and the rest of your stuff is in the truck. Sir, you ready?"

Tears forming in her eyes, Kizzy slid out his arms. It was still early morning, and the sun had just risen, but already she could tell the difference in the land as if it was rolling under their feet. "Do you know if any of the townspeople have left?"

He ushered her toward the bikes. "I think about half of the town has taken our warning seriously. You'll be happy to know those who considered you a friend are moving north. The baker, nursery owner, that coffee shop lady. I told each of them where we will be going yesterday." He stopped beside his bike. "We're driving through town on the way out. Are you going to be okay with that?" he asked, brushing a strain of her hair back.

"I'll be fine as long as I have you and my family next to me."

Running Wolf placed the helmet on her head. "This has a two-way microphone in it so we can speak to each other. Dark Horse and Sun Bull will hear us also. They will be right beside us as we ride out. Has your family already started out?" He donned his helmet and climbed on the bike, holding it steady while she joined him.

"Yeah, most of them are heading toward Canada, but the he-men of my family insisted on going with us."

"Let me guess. Your brother?" Running Wolf lifted his hand. Everyone around them started their bikes. "Your uncles and some of your cousins."

Kizzy wrapped her arms around him tight, feeling the vibrations of the bike. "Okay this is almost as strong as my..." Her face heated. To her left, Dark Horse was grinning like a fiend. "Never mind."

Running Wolf squeezed her leg as they pulled out on Highway 224. She looked over her shoulder once more at site of her magical wedding night.

"It will always be in our hearts, and we have your pictures to help us remember," Running Wolf said as if sensing her mood.

"I know, but it feels like part of me is being left behind." She rested her head on his back, watching as they drove through town. Half the businesses were closed, and Kizzy swore that the remaining business owners were glaring at them. "Do you get the feeling we are not welcome here anymore?"

"It will only get worse now," Running Wolf said as they finally moved out of the town and headed toward a new destination.

Kizzy took one last quick glimpse back at the city that had been her home. The buildings behind her shook. "Running Wolf do you feel that?"

"Yes, it seems it's starting already. Hold on." The wind ripped by as they raced away from the doomed city. Her heart sank as the three-story bank building swayed and started to crumble.

"It's almost as if she waited for us to leave," Kizzy murmured.

"The Great Mother is giving us a chance, and we must listen and watch for her signs, now more than ever."

After leaving 224, they drove for two hours. No one said anything much as they drove down I71 until Running Wolf pulled off at an exit with a coffee house. Kizzy slipped off the bike. "We're going to have to find a hotel with a hot tub when we stop." She took her helmet off, shaking her head, hoping she didn't have helmet hair.

"We won't be staying at a hotel. We'll be camping out, Little Gypsy. But I promise to rub you down." He took the helmet and kissed her hard. "Did I mention I can do amazing things with my hands?"

Her face heated as she remembered the number of times he'd slid his fingers into her.

"You remember last night." He nipped her lip. "Let's get something to drink and some food before we take off again."

Kizzy placed her hand into his, noticing the small store across the street. "I'd like to run over there. Would you order me a large coffee with double cream while I check it out?"

"I'll come with you." Running Wolf waved Sun Bull over. "Get us two large coffees and some type of scones if they have any. Blueberry?"

"Blueberry would be great." She squeezed his hand.

Her brother and Stephan followed them to the store.

"Shopping already?" Mason teased, and she slapped him.

"I want cameras to take pictures so we'll remember," Kizzy said as Running Wolf opened the door for her. She stepped inside.

"Hey, I was only kidding." Mason placed a kiss on the top of her head as she adjusted to the light in the store. She took in all the homemade things. Her brother was right. She would have bought many things in this store.

Kizzy stopped at the postcard rack. "Perfect." She selected five cards from the rack showing the town they were in then approached a rack of handmade quilts. A stunning dark-green and blue one called to her, and she stroked the soft fabric.

The saleslady approached her. "My grandma just finished that one today. Said someone coming here would want it. I'm Nella Greenleif, and over there is my grandma, Bertha." Kizzy lost track of the conversation, her eyes glued to the scene on a small TV mounted on the back wall.

The woman moved to stand next to her. "It's so sad. That whole town gone. From what they have been saying, over seven hundred may have been killed."

A strong arm wrapped around her. "Do you have everything? I want to get on the road as soon as possible." He kissed the top of her head. "There was nothing we could have done." He grabbed the quilt she had been touching and headed to the counter.

"Hey, you don't have to do that," Kizzy said, grabbing several cameras from a display rack.

Running Wolf laid the cameras and postcards on top of the quilt. "Yes, I do. My gift to you." He kissed her forehead as the older woman grinned at them both.

"You need this, too," the older woman said, laying a pink-and-purple baby blanket next to their purchases.

Kizzy stared. "What?"

"You will have a cute little girl soon. She'll need this." She put their items in a bag and pushed it toward them.

"But..."

Running Wolf placed his hand on her back. "Thank you, ma'am. How much do I owe you?"

"Hey, I'm paying for this." Kizzy tried to step around him, but Running Wolf held her at his side.

"You are my wife, and I take care of you as it should be." He pulled out a credit card, but the woman waved it away.

"No, this is for you, my gift. We will be meeting you later. I already have my granddaughter and son packing. We'll be leaving next week for Canada." The old woman took Kizzy's hand and squeezed it. "We are bringing three families with us and are canning all our produce and will ship it all up there before we go. We will be there to help you both."

"You thought we would be the only one to hear the Great Mother." Running Wolf bowed his head to the woman. "We thank you for your gift and will see you in a few weeks."

"Do you believe her?" Once outside, Kizzy placed her hand on her stomach. "Could I be pregnant already?" she asked, stumbling over the curb.

Running Wolf grabbed Kizzy around her waist, keeping his wife from falling flat on her face. Behind them, Mason snorted.

"You'll have to just wait to find out, but at least we know what you will be having." Stephan opened to the door to the coffee shop.

Running Wolf took a deep breath, enjoying the scent of fresh coffee. "I hate to say it, but this is one thing I will miss."

Her face scrunched up, and he could almost hear the wheels turning in her head. "I have an old coffee pot Mom and Dad used over the campfire. Maybe we can get some canned coffee and tea to store." Kizzy spun around and headed back outside. "I need to go to the bike."

"What are you doing?" Running Wolf followed her.

"I need my pad of paper. It's in my backpack."

"A pad of paper?"

"I always carry a pad of paper, a small notebook with me. Everything is so up in the air, I am afraid I'll leave my head next." Kizzy opened her backpack and pulled out her purse. "I'm afraid if I don't write things down, I forget them."

"Come on, Little Gypsy. Let's get our coffee," Running Wolf said.

They settled at a table by the window where, for the next thirty minutes, Kizzy showed him her little notebook-calendar.

"Little Gypsy, what is this payment thing you have noted each month? It says hospital? Were you in the hospital?"

"It's nothing, just something I've been paying on, but it's almost paid off."

Her brother caught her gaze. "I don't remember you being in the hospital. Answer your husband's question." Mason grabbed her book out of her hand, flipping through it.

"Give that back. You have no right." Kizzy reached for it, but he held it out of her reach.

Running Wolf snatched the book from her brother, daring him to say anything. "Now, tell us what happened, please." He handed her back the little book.

She stuffed the book into her purse and tore her scone apart, stuffing a piece in her mouth. "It was about two weeks after Mom and Dad died and the first time I was on my own. I wasn't paying attention to those around me at one of the rest stops when one of those crazy people found me. I got roughed up a little bit. Let's just say I was lucky the police rode in, but I ended up in the hospital overnight."

"Why didn't you call me?" Mason was furious.

Kizzy shrugged. "All my life everyone had been protecting me. I needed to handle this. Plus, I wasn't staying there. I was just driving by the city, so I really didn't see any reason to call. A couple cracked ribs and bruises I can deal with. You had your own problems getting your family situated."

Mason took her hands. "Little sister, I don't want to lose you. When Mom and Dad were killed, I knew I had to make sure I didn't lose you, too. Don't do that again. Something happens, you tell us." Mason glanced at her husband.

"There will be no more secrets, right?" Running Wolf said as Sun Bull came back into the dinner. "Eat up, Little Gypsy. The bikes are all filled, time to roll out."

"I'm done, a scone and a half is enough for me. Let me run to the bathroom first." Kizzy stood up and stretched. "Now you guys can talk about me." She made her way through the throngs of his people and the locals.

"That one is going to have to be watched always." Soaring Eagle came up to him and patted his shoulder. "But she has a heart of gold."

Chapter Fifteen

"The first day my wife stands beside me, we look towards the future with nervousness, but together we can face anything." Running Wolf, President White Buffalo MC

Kizzy ground her teeth and glared at the nutcase in front of her. She would never be allowed to take a walk by herself again if this jerk wouldn't allow her to pass. "Please, sir. My husband and family are waiting for me. Kindly step out of the way," she asked for the sixth time.

The creep had one front tooth missing, greasy hair, a bald spot on the top of his head, and dead eyes. He took a step toward her, and she backed up. "You're the one sent for me," he said before reaching out and trying to grab her arm.

"I don't think so." She yanked away and kicked the man square in the balls, sick and tired of the creeps thinking she was there for them. When the man dropped to his knees, she scooted around him, but he grabbed onto her leg, bringing her down.

The air rushed out of her chest, and her head hit the floor hard. "Running Wolf," she yelled, tired of this crap and this man who was now grabbing her ass. "Get off of me!" Kizzy tried to kick the man again, but he covered her legs, his stinky breath on her face.

"Now you just earned—"

Running Wolf lifted the man off of her and threw him down the hallway of the coffeehouse.

Dark Horse lifted her up and flinched. "You're going to have a nice goose egg, Kizzy. Let's get you some ice on that knot. Did he hurt you anywhere else?" he asked, checking her out.

"Other than needing a damn shower and the breath being

79

knocked out of me, I'm fine. God, why do I draw the creepy ones?" She pulled her shirt down and pushed back into the bathroom, needing to at least wash her hands. "Make sure Running Wolf doesn't kill the guy. We don't need to be stuck here any longer than necessary."

Dark Horse stepped into the bathroom behind her while she washed her hands and face.

"You know you are in the lady's bathroom, right?"

He leaned against the wall and crossed his arms, giving her one of those scary biker stares.

She laughed. "You really believe that look is going to scare me?"

"I'm fine, and the police have him." Running Wolf stepped into the bathroom, nodding to Dark Horse. "You okay, Little Gypsy?" he asked, brushing her hair away from the bump on her head.

"Yeah. Thanks for getting here so fast." She dried her hands, threw the paper towel in the garbage, and hugged him tight. "Let's get out of this place, please?"

He scooped her up in his arms. "From now on, you take a guard with you wherever you go." Running Wolf kissed the top of her head.

"How did I know you were going to say that?" She kissed his chest, resting her head on it.

"Because he's right. You need someone to watch your back with everything going on. I mean it, Kizzy. You can't fight this." Mason met them in the dining room.

All eyes focused on her, and she hated it. "Running Wolf, get me out of here."

He shook his head. "You have to speak with the police, Kizzy."

So, for the next hour, she sat in Running Wolf's arms, holding an ice bag on her head, as the police officer took her statement. By the time he left, she was mentally drained.

"Can we go now?" She put the ice bag on the table.

"I don't know if we should be riding with your bump on your head," he said, studying her wound. "Red Hawk, take a look at her?"

"No, he is not going to do anything. I'm fine. If you want to stop early later on fine, but we need to get out of this town now." She shivered.

Red Hawk sat near them. "What is it, Kizzy?"

"I don't know, but we need to move on. Someone is waiting for us. Plus, we have to meet the rest of your group in Louisville."

"Promise you'll tell me if you get dizzy or need to stop?" Running Wolf asked.

"I promise. Can we go?"

He stood, not releasing his hold on her. "Let's get out of here." Running Wolf said as everyone started to move toward the door.

Thirty minutes later, Kizzy took a deep breath. The land around them as they moved down I-71 was stunning. The nervousness was gone, and she could breathe again. She didn't know why it was so important to leave that town, but it was.

"You going to tell me what is wrong?" Running Wolf's voice came through the helmet speaker.

"I honestly don't know. It was just a very heavy feeling, like someone was sitting on my chest. We have to keep moving or something will happen, not in our favor, either."

"You think it has something to do with my woman?" Dark Horse, who rode next to them, asked.

"I have no idea, and that is why it's driving me crazy. If I knew what was going to happen or had a vision it would be easier, but I hate when this happens."

Running Wolf reached back and squeezed her leg. "You do what you can, Little Gypsy. That is all that matters. How are you feeling?"

"I'm fine, really. The fresh air is helping a lot. I'll be fine." She tried to reassure Running Wolf and the others who were listening. "Do you really think I'm pregnant? Are you okay with us having a little girl first?"

"A little girl who looks just like her momma," Running Wolf said.

Dark Horse snorted. "And you'll have every boy around sniffing after her, too."

"Joke away, because I have a feeling you are going to have a load of children, and I can see them running around driving you crazy, too," Kizzy teased.

Sun Bull rose on their other side. He was a quiet one.

"Sun Bull, how many children do you want?" she asked, trying to drag him into the conversation.

"None," he stated.

"Okay. I hate to break it to you, but life has a way of changing our minds."

Finally, he turned his gray eyes on her. "I think not." Sun Bull returned his attention to the road.

"Drop it, Little Gypsy," Running Wolf said.

"Fine. I'm sorry if I offended him. I was just trying to get to know your friends." She placed her palm on her leg.

Running Wolf reached back, bringing her hand around him again. "I know you're trying, baby, but give it time. You don't need to rush. Let things play out."

Kizzy was pushing it, but she wanted to fit in. Not always be stirring up trouble with her abilities. Sometimes, Kizzy wished she could just be normal, but that wasn't going to happen.

Running Wolf took a deep breath. Kizzy was hurt, but his friend Sun Bull was a man unto himself. He was smart and a fierce protector of his friends, but he was also very quiet, studying everything around him.

"Tell me about your mom and dad, Little Kizzy," he asked, trying to change the subject, but also wanting to know more about his wife.

"Mom liked to work outside in the garden, and she'd go into the forest, planting things, food hidden, so if something ever happened, there would be plants. That's how I knew to do this for Rose and her family. I don't know how many campgrounds around the US now have wild lettuce, squash, corn, and tomatoes. Dad used to laugh at her, teasing her till we went back a few years later to a couple of those sites. Sure enough, the seeds she had planted had taken off. It was amazing. Even Uncle Stephan was impressed, and, believe me, it takes a lot to impress that man." Mom had a green thumb. She would talk with her plants while pulling weeds.

"My dad was smart as a tack. Half of our family allowed him to invest their money in the stock exchange. We were lucky Dad had a sense something wasn't right and pulled out most of it before the market crashed. Every single one of my uncles is very well off. I used to have a nice nest egg, but I'm afraid half of it was stolen a month after I left home when my folks died."

He stiffened. "Who stole it?" The thought of someone taking what should have been hers had him furious.

"Money isn't important. What hurt the worst was Henry took my mother's ring. It was one of the few things I had of hers, and I have no idea where he is now. I even checked the pawnshops near where he lived. I guess we all have been suckers at some point in our lives. We can sit around moping about it or move forward, even though it hurts." She fidgeted behind him. "That is when I moved to Milan, Ohio. I loved the area, and everyone seemed so nice. Guess my judgment isn't the greatest."

"Hey, you picked me," Running Wolf growled.

"It's more like you took me, dear sir." Kizzy giggled. "Even though I do have to admit I did find the whole degrading thing kind of sexy."

Both Dark Horse and Sun Bull groaned.

"You do know his head is going to swell so big it won't fit in his helmet?" Dark Horse said.

"Hell, he'll puff out his chest and beat it next," Sun Bull added.

"Watch it you two," he snapped.

"Tell me how all of you met. I know you're not from the same area," Kizzy said.

"I'm not as gifted as you are, or Soaring Eagle, but, under his teaching, I did seek my vision quest. We usually don't speak of this, but I'll tell you. There were flashes of things I didn't understand: the white buffalo, a horse, motorcycle, and flashes of our people suffering. With Soaring Eagle's wisdom and a few friends, we knew what we had to do. Each man who joined came because he, too, had been given some sort of sign. At first, there was tension and disagreements among us, but our one purpose remains the same: to pick our people back up and lend a hand no one else has offered."

"I'm amazed at all that you have done. It seems each of you has a place in your group to help those who need it. It's like an organized company." Kizzy told him.

She was right. Each member of their group had a specialty, but it was more than that. It was as if he and his men had connected the first time he had met his them. Running Wolf couldn't explain something he didn't understand himself.

"I'm sorry, Little Gypsy. I don't feel as I'm doing the experience justice with the way I'm describing it. Meeting each man was an experience in itself. Like they belonged. I guess it was the only time you could say I had a little gift handed to me because I'd never experienced anything like it until I heard your voice."

"Do you know when I knew you were going to be a part of my life? The day I saw your picture on your website. It's the only reason I stayed where I was so long, or I would have left long ago. I usually don't ignore my visions, but I knew in my heart I had to wait. Talk about a conflict of emotions and my gift, but in the end I chose my heart." She locked her arms around him.

"And I let you get hurt," Running Wolf growled.

"No, Soaring Eagle showed me there was nothing you could have done. That it was predestined. I had to prove I was good enough to stand beside the warrior who would save us."

"Bullshit!" He glared at her. "You're too good for me. I'm not a saint, Kizzy. Far from it. I have the soul of an old warrior, and, believe me, I wanted to skin those two assholes alive," he said. "Maybe we balance each other out. Where you are honest, have a heart of gold, and are nurturing, I'm the opposite, a warrior. Burn me once, you don't get another chance."

Chapter Sixteen

"The ground opens up, taking the earth we once walked upon. Will it take us next?"
Sun Bull, White Buffalo MC

Kizzy snorted, staring out at the landscape. She sure didn't feel like a damn saint. Hell, half of the thoughts in her head were downright naughty. "Do you have other things packed in the truck?" she asked Running Wolf.

"No, everything I need is in the saddle bags, why?"

"Just wondering?" Knowing what she would be searching for in Louisville, all she had to do was sneak away from everyone if she could. Maybe she could take her brother, but nope, he'd open his mouth to her husband.

"Your woman is planning something," Dark Horse said. "I swear I can see the gears moving inside that little head of hers."

"Of course I'm thinking. With everything that is going on, how can one not?" Kizzy flipped down the visor on the helmet.

"Oh no. She's hiding her face now," Dark Horse teased her.

"Just wait. We'll see who's laughing when I find your mate, buster," she grumbled.

"Knock it off." Running Wolf eased up on the throttle. "What the hell?"

Kizzy tried to peek around him but couldn't.

"Do you think we can get around it?" Running Wolf came to a complete stop on the highway.

Cars had stopped, too.

"What's wrong?" she asked.

Dark Horse parked his bike, and he and Sun Bull walked ahead.

85

"There are cars stopped about a half block ahead. They'll find out what's wrong. If we need to, we can take a back route around this." He took off his helmet and got off the bike.

"Wow, never seen anything like that," Kizzy said. "That's a news chopper flying over us, so whatever it is must be pretty big." She pulled off her helmet. "Look at all that dust on the right shoulder."

"Get your helmets on and turn around. The ground is crumbling into a massive sink hole," Dark Horse yelled, racing toward them. He jumped on his bike.

Kizzy jerked her helmet back on and scrambled onto the bike behind Running Wolf. Sun Bull and Dark Horse pulled ahead of them, and the others followed as they raced back the way they came.

"We'll get off at that last exit and find out what is going on. We'll plan our way from there." Running Wolf said.

No one said another word as they raced toward the exit marked West Chester. Kizzy did not like the looks of things. They needed to get to Texas immediately. Things were starting to happen around them too fast.

"We need more time. I thought we had close to five years before this would happen."

"We still might have time. Remember, it's not going to happen overnight. But you never know. Maybe the Great Spirit wanted us to take a different route. Our group has never been one for planning. We go where people need our help, Little Gypsy. Maybe there is someone here in need. We don't question." Running Wolf drew her hands around his middle and patted them. "Don't worry. We'll get there in time."

"We might as well eat lunch here, so we don't have to stop again," Kizzy said.

Running Wolf finally found a diner called First Watch. Kizzy got off the bike, shaking her head when taking off her helmet. Fire trucks and police cars raced by them, heading back the way they'd come.

Running Wolf grabbed the GPS and map from the saddlebag. "Come on, Little Gypsy. Let's get something to eat and figure this out."

Kizzy stepped inside the diner filled with Running Wolf's men. "You know we're going to have to leave a big tip for the poor ladies."

"You're a sweetie. Come on. Sun Bull has a table for us." Running Wolf led them through the tables of his men and the townspeople.

Taking a seat across from Dark Horse, Running Wolf sat beside her, pulling her chair over so she was almost sitting in his lap. "Now, tell why you were asking if I had anything else in the truck? What do you think I need?"

"Nothing important. Just wondered." The waitress set a glass of water in front of her, and she lifted it and took a sip.

"Her face is a nice shade of pink. She'll never be a great poker player," Dark Horse said.

"Keep it up and I'll make sure I find a perfect voodoo doll for your butt. Wouldn't it be funny to see you hopping around in front of your woman without knowing why, the first time you meet her."

"Kizzy has a little bit of temper, or maybe she just can't take a good ribbing," Dark Horse said, leaning back in his chair.

Tucking her napkin in her lap, Kizzy smiled. "Oh revenge can be fun. Just ask Mason. He usually bore the brunt of mine."

Mason proceeded to enlighten both Running Wolf and Dark Horse about how she had no fear of snakes, but something was off. Her stomach knotted, her hands started to sweat, and she swore someone was waiting for her.

Her brother touched her arm, scaring the living shit out of her. She jumped and almost fell out of her chair. If it hadn't been for her husband catching her, Kizzy's backside would have held a nice bruise.

"What?" Mason asked.

"You know, you are really a pain in the ass. I don't know yet, so leave me alone," she snapped and reached for her water, but her hand shook so badly so she gave up on that. However, Running Wolf was there, lifting the glass to her mouth.

"We're here for you. Just tell us what's up when you can," he said into her ear, setting the glass down after she took a drink. "Want me to order you a burger?"

She nodded, slowly scanning the room, but nothing was out of place. Kizzy drummed her fingers on the table, and glanced outside. "Running Wolf."

Running Wolf's gaze followed Kizzy's, and he snarled. "Let's go, guys, Kizzy stay behind us," he ordered then stalked toward the crazy man with the knife carrying a blood-soaked blanket. It was wrapped around what he thought might be a small child...and he only hoped it was alive.

A man from the diner stepped outside with them. "That's Mark Sanders, a vet, but also an ex heroin addict. His wife was pregnant with a baby girl. Looks like she might have delivered."

"You talk to him while we try and get around him. We need him distracted so we can get to that baby before he can hurt it," Running Wolf said. "Dark Horse, you go to the left and I'll go right." Before he could, Sun Bull took the right side.

For the next thirty minutes, the man from the diner talked to the stranger holding the knife, but the man said nothing. They had been told by the owner of the diner that the police were about ten minutes away but were finally coming.

"You need to move now. He's not going to last till the police get here," Kizzy said. "Maybe if I talked to him." She stepped around him.

"Damn it, Kizzy." Running Wolf dragged her back into his embrace. "You can do it from here."

She counted to ten. At once, Mark seemed to focus on Kizzy. He stepped forward.

"Is that your baby? Is it hurt? Do you need a doctor? My name is Kizzy, and this man behind me is my husband. Can we help you?" she asked, her voice almost musical, calming.

The man took a deep breath. "They killed my wife. I had no choice." He inched forward, his gaze moving to hers. "I tried to protect her, but I didn't get home in time." The man fell to his knees. "She told me to save the baby." He stared down at the child in his hands. "I'm dying, Kizzy. She got pregnant so she could keep a part of me, and now she won't be here to raise her.

She wanted you to have her. Before she died, my wife knew you were coming." The man laid the baby on the ground. The little girl was moving around, crying now. He reached for his phone and punched some buttons. "She wanted you to believe me. Please come get it." He dropped the knife next to him.

"Stay here, Kizzy." Running Wolf stepped forward slowly, while Sun Bull came up from behind him and kicked the knife away. Running Wolf reached out, took the phone, and handed it to Kizzy.

She pressed some buttons and held the phone up to him. What he saw made his stomach knot. The woman in the video had the Irons' mark craved on her face, her eyes were swollen shut, her lip busted open, and blood trickled out of her mouth.

A shadow fell over them. A cop and two others helped Mark stand. One carried the baby carefully to a waiting ambulance.

"Officer Neil, I know you are watching this..." The woman in the video coughed and more blood came out of her mouth. Kizzy whimpered, and Running Wolf wrapped his arms around her. "My husband did not do this. Two bikers. Not Mark's fault. Please, Miranda needs to go to the woman called Kizzy. She'll raise her right. It's my dying wish." Her head moved to the person holding the phone, her husband. "Take the baby out of me, Mark. Save her." The phone fell and they heard Mark pleading with her not to do this, but she said she had made him promise. "Even I know I'm dying, baby. Soon we'll be together, and we can watch our daughter grow to a healthy beautiful soul with this woman."

The phone video went dead, and Kizzy tried to give it to the police officer, but she was shaking so much she almost dropped it, twice.

"Here, let me take it. I gather you are Kizzy?" the officer asked. "You recognized something in the video? I think the two of you need to come with me, please. My name is Neil Brown."

Dark Horse and Sun Bull followed them to the police station where, for the next two hours, Officer Neil questioned them both, separately, which really pissed Running Wolf off. He didn't like leaving Kizzy alone with anyone.

"I've answered all your questions, but I would really like to see my wife, please," he said.

The officer sat back in his chair. "She's being brought in here. So you really believe this Iron group did this, Mr. Running Wolf?"

"Yes. I don't know why, but it seems the president of the Irons knows we are coming, and I'm afraid it was a warning to me. If you—"

The door flew open and another officer rushed in.

"Mark is dead. We thought he laid down to get some rest in the ambulance, but the paramedics are saying his heart stopped and they couldn't get it going again."

Neil rose. "I knew it wouldn't take long. He had been holding on for her. He had brain cancer, and the doctors didn't know how he could be walking around."

Kizzy came in and approached him, wrapping his arms around him. "He's gone. Mark has joined his wife. What do we do?"

Running Wolf placed a kiss on her forehead. "We get the things we'll need for our new daughter," he said. "Do we know how long the paperwork will take, Officer? We really need to get to Texas."

"Two days, max. I'll make sure of it. The judge is already going over the tape and crime scene now. Check into a hotel room, and I'll get word to you as soon as I know. Thank you, both of you. You are free to go."

Chapter Seventeen

"Each child has a soul, seeking knowledge and love. It's up to us to share the best of us with it." Running Wolf, President White Buffalo MC

Kizzy stared in the bathroom mirror. Running Wolf had gone all out and gotten them a suite with a huge garden tub, and, right now, Kizzy couldn't wait to climb in. She was going to be a mother. No, she was now a mother.

She turned on the faucet and cupped some water in her hands, splashing it into her face, washing it. When she lifted her head, Running Wolf stood behind her, undoing the braid in her hair. "Everyone is settling in. We'll be driving the truck and towing my bike." He leaned down and kissed the side of her neck. "Maybe after the soak in the tub, we'll get to check out some stores and pick up baby things before we meet everyone for supper."

"Do you really believe we'll be given Miranda? Are we ready for a child? We just came together, and that was under stress." She so didn't feel like she deserved this little girl.

Running Wolf placed his fingers under her chin, adding a little pressure until Kizzy looked into his eyes. "We will give her a chance to live, love her, and tell her how much her parents loved her to give her life. All we can do is give our best and hope the child takes the good and learns from our bad habits, but we will be beside her as long as we can. Trust your heart, Little Gypsy." He kissed her nose before sweeping her up in his arms and carrying her toward the tub.

Slowly, he lowered her feet to the floor, his attention never leaving her. Running Wolf stepped back. "Strip, Little Gypsy, and get into the tub." His voiced dropped, and the sexual tension rose. "I want to make love to my wife."

It took her seconds to get her clothes off because Kizzy wanted the same thing. Kizzy stepped into the warm, bubbling water. At once, the pulsing jets worked their magic on her muscles. She laid her head back against the rim of the tub. Running Wolf stripped out of his clothes and joined her.

He sank down next to her and dragged her up onto his body. "Do you know how beautiful you are? I could just sit all day and stare at what the Great Mother has given me."

His kisses were like a drug Kizzy could never get enough of. She slid her arms around his neck and opened her mouth for him. His tongue slid up and down hers, as if memorizing each little bump and line. When he curled his tongue as if trying to hug hers, she moaned, grabbing onto his now loose hair.

He slid his hand down her wet body. Lifting her hips, he broke their kiss. "Are you wet for me, Little Gypsy?"

Kizzy licked his bottom lip. "I'm in water. Yes, I'm wet," she teased.

"Put me in you, Kizzy," he ordered. He was thick and large, at least to her.

She pumped her hand up and down, hearing his gasp, but too soon he grabbed her wrist.

"I'm too close," he ground out.

"Party pooper.," S lifted then lowered herself on him. He stretched her, but there was no pain, just pleasure as he slid inside her body, joining them. "So amazing."

Running Wolf cupped her breasts before, sucking a nipple into his mouth, nipping and scraping his teeth across it. "I'd like these to be pierced soon," he said, releasing it. "I'd love to put clamps and weights on them. Your body is so sensitive to my touch."

He wrapped his arms around her and flipped them in the water, sloshing some of it over the edge of the tub. "Grab the rim behind you," he growled as he lifted her legs and placing them over his shoulder.

Kizzy couldn't believe how much deeper her husband got with her legs lifted. She swore he touched the edge of her inside, the little pain only bringing her closer to the edge. "Harder!" she pleaded, her eyes closing as his thrusts became quicker and harder.

They would have a mess to clean, up, but, right now, his possession of her was complete. There would never be another man in her life, just her husband. Her body trembling, she opened her eyes and focused on the warrior between her legs.

"I love you," she screamed as her orgasm exploded. Her toes curled, muscles cramped as his warm seed filled her, his orgasm just as powerful.

Gently, Running Wolf took one leg lifting it off his shoulder, placing a kiss on her leg as he rubbed the muscles before lowering it into the water.

She moaned, her body feeling like Jell-O. "I can't move," she grumbled, releasing the rim of the tub and lowering her arms under the water.

"You're bleeding." He lifted her hand and licked a trail of blood from her finger. "I think there is a rough edge on the tub." He reached over, ran his fingertip along the edge.

"Damn it. You could have been hurt worse. This thing is sharp." Running Wolf got out of the tub and rummaged through his bag.

She sat up. "What are you doing?"

"We need to clean that so it doesn't get infected." With some peroxide and cotton balls, he waited for her. "Come on, out of the tub, Little Gypsy. I want to wrap that finger."

"But I didn't get to soak." She pouted but realized he wasn't going to budge when he gave her that look again.

"Fine, but tonight I get to soak, dammit." She stood and grabbed a towel from the rack above the tub.

"We'll be getting a new room. I won't risk you hurting yourself with that thing poking out like that." Running Wolf applied peroxide before he reached for the Band-Aid he had placed on the dresser. "There, now why don't you get dressed and we'll go to the hospital and see the little one before we go shopping for her." He leaned over and kissed her.

"Do you think they'll let us hold her?" Kizzy asked, opening her bag and searching her clothes. She pulled out a dark-blue skirt and a white peasant blouse to go with it.

"I'm sure they will." He stared down at the clothes she'd picked out. "Why do I get the feeling this outfit is going to have me moaning, too?"

"I have no idea. Maybe you're just a sex fend," she teased, pulling out her blue panties and bra. "Now, if you will excuse me, I'll get ready." She stood on tiptoe and placed a kiss on his cheek. "Thanks for coming into my life, Running Wolf." Grabbing her clothes, she moved toward the bathroom. Knowing he watched her, she dropped the towel right before stepping into the bathroom and shutting the door.

"You, Little Gypsy, do not play fair," Running Wolf yelled, his cock hardening again. He heard her laughter as he grabbed his jeans. It would be a bitch stuffing his cock in them, but he would do it.

He couldn't wait to meet their new daughter. He just wished they were already on their way to their destination, but he would not leave his friend hanging. They'd take care of the threat then proceed on to their new home.

"Running Wolf, are we going to stop by your home to get your things before we move up to Canada?" Kizzy came out of the bathroom brushing her hair.

"Come here." He held out his hand for the brush. "Allow me the pleasure."

"Are you having difficulties there?" she asked, pointing at the stiff cock poking out of his jeans.

"I have a feeling I'm going to be hard all the time when it comes to my wife, especially when she wears clothes that enhance her beautiful body." He proceeded to brush her long, thick hair. "Yes, I think we're all going to have to pack up our belongings. I'll talk to Dark Horse about his house after we hit Texas and settle things there."

Someone pounded on the door.

"Great."

"You go fix yourself. I'll get it." She reached toward the door, but he wrapped his arm around her and pulled her back.

"Oh no, you don't. The way my luck's been going, there will be some nutjob there." He painfully zipped his jeans up and grabbed his black T-shirt. He checked out the peephole. Officer Neil stood there. "You're lucky." He moved away from the window to see his wife glaring at him.

"I take it it's okay to open the damn door now?" she snapped and did so. "Come on in, Officer Neil. Is there some news?"

Neil whistled, checking out his woman when he stepped into the room. Running Wolf suppressed the urge to deck him.

"Judge Anderson, who took the case, wants to meet with you both before you sign the papers. You'll also need your Ids," Neil explained.

Running Wolf grabbed his wallet out of the desk drawer as a

man and woman came into the room. The woman set a briefcase on their small table. Running Wolf knew Judge Anderson was sizing them both up.

"First, I'd like to thank you both for trying to help Mark," the judge said, sitting at the table. "I had to deal personally with him a few times since he came back from Iraq. We knew he didn't have long to live, but to take the love of his life away from him before...and to have to save his child this way." The judge sighed. "It's no way for anyone to suffer like that."

"My license still has my maiden name. We were recently married, and I haven't had a chance to get a new one. Kizzy stepped forward, placing her license on the table, and touched the judge's shoulder. "I'm deeply sorry for everyone in this situation. Violence never leaves anyone better off and it affects more than we know."

"My wife's parents were murdered a few years ago, so she understands the child's position and will be able to help when the time comes." Running Wolf set his license next to hers and wrapped his arms around her.

The judge studied Kizzy for a few seconds. "You have a gift just like Mark's wife had. Miranda will be in good hands." The judge looked at him. "I take it you've already had strangers come up to her? It took everything in Mark, with Neil's help, to protect his wife. She also told us our world as we know it will be changing soon. Is it true?"

Soaring Eagle stepped in the room. "It is. This man's wife wasn't the only one gifted if I'm not mistaken."

The judge smiled at the medicine man. "Yes, but it does not hurt to make sure before I place an innocent child into their hands."

"Of course. You are making a stand here?" Soaring Eagle took a seat across from the judge.

"I'm too old to go moving around, and my wife isn't in good health, so I'll make do with what I can here. A few of us have already started preparing. If we are lucky, we will be spared. Do you have one of those old-fashion CB radios yet?"

"No," Running Wolf said. "But we should probably pick one up. We have business in Texas, and then we'll be heading North up into Canada. You are welcome to join us if you change your mind. Soaring Eagle has identified four places where we will station ourselves."

"I'm sure there will be a few safe havens on the North American continent." The judge handed their licenses to the lady who took all the information down and returned them along with a stack of papers. "I'll need your signatures. You first, sir, then your wife.

"It will take strong men and women to make it through what is coming. It has already started here in Ohio, and I've heard a few other states are having troubles, too. From what I can make out, the more polluted areas will be affected first."

Soaring Eagle tapped his fingers on the table. "I had a feeling that would happen. We must get our business in Texas finished quickly. I have a feeling soon the ground will separate, so travel from the south to the north will not be easy."

The judge stood and stretched. "I have four CB radios. My father was a collector. I will give you one, but as you travel, pick up what you can. I suggest purchasing four-wheel drive vehicles when you reach your destination. Bikes will also be good to make quick trips." The judge picked up his briefcase. "My wife is a list person. I'll have her copy her list of things she believes we need."

Running Wolf snorted. "I'm just learning my Little Gypsy is the same way. We're all going to need help eventually." He rubbed his chin on the top of Kizzy's head. "You know, I might let Dark Horse take the truck, and we can purchase an SUV now. With the child and all, it might be better. We can haul a trailer behind it."

"I'll send Dark Horse in to you." Soaring Eagle moved to the door with the judge. "If you wouldn't mind, I would like to check out the place you have picked out. I might offer some suggestions?"

As they reached the door, Running Wolf called after them, "Let's all meet at the hotel for dinner tonight."

The judge nodded and they stepped outside.

The woman rose and handed him an envelope. "In there you have all the papers you'll need for Miranda. She now has the last name of Wolf. Did I do that right?"

"Yes, that's fine."

"Will you come back this way on the way back from Texas?" Neil asked.

Running Wolf shrugged. "We will most likely be going up the coast. Why?"

"I was thinking about going with you if you don't mind. Me and my daughter. But I need time to get things together here."

"You would be welcome. I will have one of my men give you a map of where we are going," Running Wolf said.

"Thank you," Neil replied. "Be sure to take your paperwork with you to the hospital when you pick up Miranda. They will also be sending a care package to help you get started with her."

Chapter Eighteen

"How do we prepare for end of everything we know? We don't. We follow our heart and hope the Great Mother will guide us." Sun Bull, White Buffalo MC

Kizzy inhaled the baby smell of her new tiny bundle in her arms. Big blue eyes stared up at her as she held the bottle to the baby's lips. Running Wolf and she had come at the perfect time, her feeding time.

Each nurse had given her a hug with tears in her eyes, telling them how perfect they were for this special little girl, and she was special. Already, Kizzy knew the little one had been born with something extra, like her mother and her.

"We are a lot alike, are we not, Miranda, my little angel?"

"Are you sure?" He placed a kiss on her curly black hair.

"Yep, and she's going to be a looker, too. Boy, are you in trouble," she teased.

Running Wolf nipped Kizzy's ear. "Keep it up and I'll spank that cute ass of yours. Don't think I forgot you glaring at me earlier."

"Right now is not a good time to bring that up." Miranda squirmed in her arms as if sensing her mood. "Easy, little one, your mommy is just a little pissed at the overbearing man sitting next to us." She whispered, "I mean, really, I don't mind the bossiness in the bedroom, but to tell me not to open a door? Please. Your new daddy and I are going to have some words tonight.

"But don't worry when daddy gets mad. Maybe Momma needs to get some handcuffs. We can lock him in the bedroom. What do you think?" She leaned down, placing a kiss on the tiny hand that patted her nose.

"I'm glad you agree, Miranda, because our warrior is a fierce one, and we'll need all the help we can get." Kizzy slowly lifted her eyes, scanning his body, but stopped at his cock, noticing once more the outline of a very hard, long...

"Keep staring at it and I'll find a damn empty room here, Little Gypsy, and I will be the only one owning handcuffs. Now, let me hold our daughter before we have to leave."

Placing a kiss on Miranda's cheek, Kizzy handed her to Running Wolf. Then she kissed his cheek. "I mean it. We will talk about the door thing."

Her brother and uncle strode into their little waiting room as Miranda finished her bottle before they left the hospital.

"Of course, my sister has to have a child who is going to draw as much attention as she does." Mason ran his finger over her little arm. "Those big blue eyes."

Stephan nodded. "We're all going to have to make sure we have enough bullets in our guns." He smiled, though. "I heard you're going to buy a car when you leave here?"

Kizzy laughed. "Let me introduce you to the car junkies of our family. You name it, they have driven it. Just make sure it's four-wheel-drive and an automatic. I can't drive a stick." She took Miranda back and burped her.

"Nope, it's Uncle's turn to hold this beauty," Mason said, taking Miranda. "She's big for a preemie. Our little girl was only three pounds."

"She wasn't really a preemie," a nurse said, coming into the room. "Her mother was due in a week's time. I need to take the little one to see the doctor. She'll get her first set of vaccines today. You'll be able to pick her up tomorrow around ten." The nurse handed her a folder with a vaccination schedule. "Her pediatrician will take over from here."

"Running Wolf, how are we going to work with medical aspect? What if she gets sick or gets something from other people, children?" Kizzy's stomach knotted as her brother handed Miranda to the nurse.

"We have Red Hawk, but we will need more healers. Add that to your list, Little Gypsy. We'll also need to start growing herbs for Red Hawk. It might be time to start going back to natural healing because we don't know what is going to be left." He moved to her side, staring down at the list. "But most of these she'll have before then. We need to have that copied and given to Red Hawk, so he can start planning also."

For the next couple of hours, they went from dealership to dealership while Dark Horse, Running Wolf, Mason, and her uncles compared the cars until she was ready to go crazy. Tapping her foot in impatience, she noticed a Babies R Us across the street from their current location.

Yep, time to do some shopping while they argue over the car. Kizzy was inching toward the door, when Soaring Eagle blocked her path. "Going somewhere, dear?"

"Why yes I was. Would you like to accompany me to the baby store across the road to do some shopping? I think it's about time we chat, don't you?" She hooked her arm through the old man's.

"Kizzy, we'll be done here in a few minutes," Running Wolf said.

"Let's see...." She tapped her lips and cocked her head to the side. "I do believe he's said that three times already. It's eight o'clock and most stores will be closing in an hour. We haven't eaten yet either. So, you buy the car and meet us across the street when you are finished. I'm sure Soaring Eagle and I can do just fine."

"I suppose you already know which car we should get?" Running Wolf asked.

"Why, yes I do. The blue Hummer. One, it's built like a tank for added protection. Two, good off-road, and three, I like the color." She flashed him her biggest smile.

He waved the salesman over. "Start the paperwork. We're buying the blue Hummer. I'm going to take my wife across the street. When you're ready for me to sign papers, Dark Horse, come get me."

"You're going to let my sister pick the car?" Mason gaped at him.

"She has the main points down, and I was leaning toward a Humvee anyway, so why not give her the blue one? Now, if you will excuse me, I would like to help my wife pick out stuff for our daughter." Running Wolf took her other hand, and the three of them headed outside.

"So how was this place the judge is setting up?" Kizzy asked. "I'm really worried about them staying here."

Soaring Eagle patted her arm. "Rest assured, he has done well for a white man." The old medicine man laughed. "I actually teased him about it, too. He kept threatening to throw me in jail for contempt of something."

Running Wolf and Soaring Eagle went to step off the curb, but she stopped, jerking them to a halt on either side of her.

"Running Wolf," she murmured, a shiver running up her spine. "Someone is watching us."

He whistled loudly, and she jumped.

"What the hell?" She dropped his arm and smacked him in the stomach. "Don't do that. You almost gave me a heart attack."

Sun Bull, Penn, Dark Horse, and Red Hawk all came out and surrounded them.

"Well damn, that was fast." She tilted her head to toward the west. "Killers are still in the area." Kizzy checked both ways and proceeded to the store. "To the left of us, I do believe near the grocery store somewhere, but that is all I can get." She strolled along, acting like nothing was wrong. "I would really like them taken care of before we get on the road. It would give the town some peace."

Already, Dark Horse was on the phone, speaking urgently.

Running Wolf nodded. "We'll try. Let's get some shopping done while my men handle this."

"They'll kill the assholes, and we need answers, plus the town needs closure." Kizzy grabbed a cart. "I'm so going to tell their wives."

Soaring Eagle let out a belly laugh.

His wife was a vindictive one, but Soaring Eagle had taken a liking to her. The two of them were driving Running Wolf nuts and freaking the crap out of others in the store.

"Okay, stop," he said as he placed a car seat into the basket he had collected since they already filled one cart. "You two are starting to draw attention to us every time you say something about everyone that passes us. Not everyone thinks your gifts are special."

"Really? I thought it was the fact we are buying up a storm and holding the store open," she teased. "But I do believe we have enough for our little princess. We have two cases of formula, three packages of cloth diapers, and one of the disposable even though I don't like the idea of using them."

"They are biodegradable. I made sure. We'll use them only in emergencies, but I have to agree the cloth will do fine, and we have glass bottles so we can reuse these also. I think we did quite well today. Plus, we'll have the bundle the nurses are giving us." Kizzy ran her fingers over the portable bassinette.

He patted her hand. "I'll make her a bed when we get where we are going, but, for now, this will have to do."

She smiled. "I'm fine. I was just remembering the one Mason has that was ours. I think your building her one will be perfect." Kizzy pulled out her wallet at the checkout lane.

"What do you think you are doing?" He pushed the second cart up to the register.

"You bought the car. I want to buy this load of things we'll need. It will be as if her grandparents helped."

He tucked a piece of her hair back. "This is important to you?"

"Please, I want to keep them alive in my heart, and knowing their money helped with our child would mean a lot."

He kissed her cheek. "You pay for the stuff, and I'll run over and sign the papers for the car. They should be ready now. But do not leave this store till I get back."

"I'll stay with her," Sun Bull told him. "One of the Irons men is already sitting in the local jail."

"Do you think we could hit Red Lobster? I mean I know we are meeting everyone, but I would so love some fish right now, my treat. . And they have those amazing biscuits. We can get a doggy bag of those for breakfast." Kizzy bounced on her heels, her eyes got big, and she licked her lips.

"Sun Bull will let the others know where to meet us." Running Wolf kissed her again because he had to. "Red Lobster, here we come. You coming?" he asked Soaring Eagle.

"I'm with her. The biscuits are to die for," he teased, and she laughed, hugging the old man.

"You remind me of my father," Kizzy said.

The old man hugged her back. "It's my pleasure, and you remind me of the daughter I lost so long ago. So full of life and love."

Running Wolf slipped out the door, shaking his head. Soaring Eagle never mentioned his daughter to anyone, and his wife already had the old medicine man telling jokes.

"What's so funny?" Dark Horse asked as he entered the dealership.

"Kizzy has Soaring Eagle over there, laughing, telling jokes, and they're testing each other on their gifts. Do you believe that?" Running Wolf sat down and signed all the papers, and the salesman left them. "Not only that, he's talking about Crystal."

Dark Horse jerked his head up. "Really?"

"He's comparing Kizzy to her." They strolled outside and

accepted the keys from the salesman.

"You have a magical person in your wife, my friend. She heals the souls of those most affected by past tragedies." Dark Horse popped the hatch when they parked in front of the store.

"I know, and I have a feeling our daughter is going to be just as powerful as Kizzy." Running Wolf got out of the car and grabbed the cart from Kizzy while Dark Horse took Soaring Eagle's.

After the items were loaded, Running Wolf drove to the Red Lobster he had seen, Sun Bull and Dark Horse following. "Neil and the Judge are meeting up with us, while we eat. His honor is bringing his wife, too. She'll have all the lists she's put together for you." Running Wolf pulled into the packed restaurant. Half the parking spots were filled with bikes from his group.

"What did you do, call everyone in?" she asked.

"We usually eat one meal together, and I have to admit we might as well enjoy what we can. Plus, we need to discuss a few things, so I had my men reserve the back room for all of us." Running Wolf came around to open her door.

"Gentleman, after all," Kizzy teased.

"In public only, baby." He wrapped his arm around her. "Tonight, I'll show you my true colors."

"You mean these?" She traced the emblem of the White Buffalo on the back of his leather duster. "You are going to have to tell me the White Buffalo story."

"I think it's time all of us heard the story again," Soaring Eagle said. He and Dark Horse accompanied them toward the entrance where Sun Bull and Penn waited.

"And let me guess, I get to tell it?" Running Wolf asked.

"You are the president, are you not?" Soaring Eagle didn't even look back at him.

"Oh good, I love a story while we eat," Kizzy said. "And you have such a deep loud voice, too, so everyone will hear you." She shivered in his arms.

He slid his hand down to her ass, cupping her cheek, and dropped his voice another notch. "Tonight, Little Gypsy, I'll tap this."

If he hadn't been holding onto her, she would have fallen flat on her ass. He wouldn't trade his passionate wife for anyone or anything.

Chapter Nineteen

"The telling of a story, to us, is relaying our history, letting our children know who we are." Running Wolf, President White Buffalo MC

Kizzy took a deep breath, sitting back and scanning around her. In a short time, all this would be gone. She might not get food like this again, unless she knew how to cook it. She would start gathering recipes that would be different and easy to make when times became hard.

"Looks like I'm not alone." A tall, thin woman with long gray hair sat down across from her. "My name is Julie Anderson. I'm Judge Anderson's wife." She patted her husband's hand while he spoke with Soaring Eagle and Running Wolf.

"I've been making lists all my life. Hello, my name is Kizzy. It's a pleasure to meet you."

The woman pulled a notebook from her bag and handed it to her. "I've made this for you. I'll have three more for you to give out in the different towns that will be created. I want to help anyone I can survive. Why do I get a feeling it's like a judgment coming our way?"

Kizzy took a drink of her sweet tea. "In some ways, I believe we are. How can we not? Look at our land and how we have destroyed it. The animals we've all but destroyed. It was only a matter of time before something happened." She held up the notebook. "Thank you for this. I still wish you two would come up north with us."

Julie sighed. "I'm afraid I am not well enough to travel. I've told my husband to go, but he's bound to stay here and make this place a haven for strangers in need." Tears shone in her eyes.

Kizzy reached over and squeezed her hand. "Be careful who you bring into your haven, Julie. Things will get bad and, in my experience, the worst of society always has a way of surviving while the good perish."

"How can one so young be so cynical?" Julie asked.

"Seeing my parents murdered and knowing it was because of my gift. So, you see, Miranda couldn't be in better care. I know what it's like to be special, and I'll be prepared."

"What my wife forgets to mention is that her aunt was not at all in her right mind. Any parent would be proud of their child, knowing she was special." Running Wolf kissed her cheek. "I'm going to keep saying it till you believe it. Put yourself in your mom's place, with Miranda in yours. Would you regret your life?"

"You know it's not the same, but no, never. In my head, I know I'm not to blame, but in my heart there will always be doubt. Now, sit and order your food so we can hear this story. I even have pen and paper ready to take notes."

"You know our history has been handed down from one generation to the next through story telling? Why start taking notes now?"

"Because I always have and it would drive me crazy not to." She frowned. "Paper. Lots and lots of notebooks." She wrote that down.

"You should see the stock pile my wife has already." Anderson chuckled, placing a kiss on the top of Julie's head. "But then again, I'd be lost without her."

"Ha, you wouldn't be able to find your robe if not for me," Julie told her husband as the waitress came to their table. "I'll have the usual, Lisa, and his honor will have?"

"No respect whatsoever, I swear. I think I'm going to have the prime rib and lobster tonight, Lisa. Change it up a little." He handed the waitress the menu. "But bring me my scotch and water please and my wife her red wine." He took a sip of water "So what is this story your husband is going to tell us?"

"What the white buffalo means to him and his people." Kizzy ordered her fish, while Running Wolf order a steak medium well just like she liked it.

"We can share," he said.

"I don't know how you know what I'm thinking," Kizzy said, kissing his cheek.

"That's easy. He's a Dom, just as Mr. Judge here is." Julie poked her husband with her fork.

Her face heated, and she fussed with the notebook.

"You made her all embarrassed. Sometimes, woman...." Judge Anderson said.

Running Wolf dragged her chair closer to his. "I'm afraid with her life endangered, moving, and getting married, we haven't really had the time to explore, but soon." Running Wolf kissed her. "You want a story." He brushed a finger down her cheek. "So beautiful, my Little Gypsy. A story before dinner it is." Running Wolf stood and cleared his throat.

The room grew quiet as all his friends turned to listen to him.

"It has come to my attention that we need to be reminded of why we are here and what we do as a group. Why we call ourselves White Buffalo."

All eyes focused on her husband. He stood tall, his long dark brown braid hanging down his back. His leather duster rested on the chair behind him. His voice was strong and powerful, perfect for storytelling.

Running Wolf had to take one more peek down at his wife, big eyes on him, ready with her little notebook and pen. He shook his head, getting those wayward thoughts out of his mind—that was for another place and time.

Right now, White Buffalo. He took a deep breath. "Long ago, before the invasion of others, our tribes were suffering. We needed food, game was scarce, so our warriors gathered to discuss what could be done. They have moved many times, only finding small game, not enough to keep them fed or clothed." He paused, allowing Kizzy to write. He ran his hand over the top of her head, loving her even more.

"I'm ready," she said. "I taught myself how to do shorthand."

"So did I, honey, so did I," Julie said, taking notes, too.

The judge snorted. "Get used to it."

"As we all know, the buffalo has always been a symbol of our sacred life and of abundance. Well, a white buffalo is the most sacred anyone can encounter." He looked at Julie. "Each religion I have found has some symbolism in its beliefs. This is one of ours."

This was the first time he had ever had to tell a story and explain it, but it was good. It felt right repeating this sacred story. "A white buffalo is born white. As it ages, the buffalo will change colors. In old times, our medicine man would know the meaning of this, as our Soaring Eagle does now. The sacred knowledge was passed down to him, from the medicine man before him. We are all very lucky to have him with us. Soaring Eagle is teaching Red Hawk the ways of our people, and in time he will take his place.

"Anyway, with the white buffalo, we were taught we don't have to struggle, that if we carefully search around us, there will always be ways to survive. There are also a few prayers we sing and dance to, which we believe help us. As we teach ourselves the appropriate things to survive. For example, all of this." Running Wolf waved at the comfortable restaurant they sat in. "Do we really need it? Can we survive without it? Yes, we can. We have lost our way, forgotten how our ancestors had to learn to survive. Well, guess what? It's time to ask our older generation to help us. They will be leading us as we all learn to survive off the land again. By teaching ourselves, we will be able to witness all that the Great Mother has left for us." Running Wolf paused to take a drink of water, allowing the women to catch up.

They signaled to him, and he continued. "I saw a white buffalo. It was in my vision quest. A sign that life's sacred loop is beginning again. Once more, we finally have purity of the mind, body, and spirit. There will be no white, black, yellow, or red, but one nation of survivors. It is a sign, an omen for the poorest people who have given up hope that change is coming. That hope and good times will once more be strong in our people. The story goes like this." Running Wolf moved through the tables of his men as he spoke. "One summer, a long time ago, our ancestors met and camped together in the Black Hills of South Dakota. The sun was blazing down on them that afternoon. People were starving. Children were too hungry to play or laugh. Two young warriors went out to try and find something for the children to eat, at least. The Lakota were a strong people, and proud. The two young warriors were hunting when a strong young beautiful woman dressed in all white appeared in front of them. 'Return to your people and tell them I'm coming,' she said." Running Wolf stopped.

Julie and Kizzy stared at him, waiting.

"This was no ordinary woman, but a holy one. She presented our men with a sacred pipe and showed our people how all things are connected. The rocks upon which we walk, the grass the animals eat, and the plants we consume to keep us going. She taught them some of the mysteries of the Earth: how to pray and follow the right path while here on this land. As she was leaving, she moved upon the ground four different times, changing color each time before turning into the white buffalo calf before she disappeared. The change of colors were white, yellow, red, and black, representing the color of man as well as the four directions north, south, west, east. When she left, great herds of buffalo surrounded our ancestors' camp. As long as they stayed true to what they'd been taught, the buffalo were plentiful. until...." Running Wolf moved to sit down.

"Now you know the history of the white buffalo."

"If I'm not mistaken, one of your brother's bison just had a white buffalo born to one of his females, didn't he?" Julie asked her husband.

The judge's head snapped up. "He did, but about three weeks ago, it was slaughtered out on the highway by someone."

"The same highway we were on?" Soaring Eagle said. "The blood of her gift was taken back. I hate to say it, but I kind of feel sorry for these Irons. They have sealed their fate."

Kizzy took a sip of water. "You know, since the Irons are in the town where we are going, where Dark Horse is to start his quest or whatever you call it, do you think maybe they know what is coming and are waiting to stop us? Or maybe they want to create a home for their families?"

Soaring Eagle leaned back in his seat. "Kizzy, my dear, you are way too smart, but you might be right." He looked at Dark Horse at the next table, pointing his knife at him. "If this is the case, you will have to cleanse the place, but.... You'll have help. I just don't know who it will be." The old man's lips moved without any sound for a moment. "Sorry, that is all I know. Sometimes this gift can be a pain, as your woman would say, Running Wolf."

They all laughed as the waitresses came into the room, bringing their dinner.

Chapter Twenty

"There is a point early in one's joining where a bond is formed between the wife and husband. The souls touching, becoming one."
Running Wolf, President White Buffalo MC

All night Kizzy had admired the way her husband handled everyone around him. While talking with others about their plans, Running Wolf seemed to know where she was at any given moment. He and his men weren't like other biker groups. At least that was what she believed.

Sure, they wore leather coats, their hair long, and rode bikes, but these men were warriors. They were out there to help the innocent and fight for those who needed the extra help. Each man had a talent, Kizzy was learning, as she had moved through the group after dinner, talking with some of his men, getting to know them. It was about time, too, since they had all come to help her and her friends.

After eating and comparing notes, Kizzy and Running Wolf said their good nights and made their way back to the hotel.

She leaned back in the shower, rinsing her hair and allowing the pulsing water to ease some of the tension in her muscles. Kizzy had asked Running to join her, but he had smiled and run one of his fingers down her cheek, saying, "I need to get things together. You go and take your time."

"What the hell did he mean by that?" Kizzy turned the water off, knowing she wouldn't find out until she stepped out of the bathroom.

Kizzy had left two towels on the rack, and her T-shirt she slept in, but now there was only one towel and no T-shirt.

The door opened to reveal Running Wolf leaning against the doorframe. He had taken off his shirt, his hair was free of his braid, and the only thing he had on were the black leather pants with the top button undone.

Running Wolf had no hair on his chest, like most full-blooded Native Americans. The man before her was on the hunt, and, from the look in his eyes, he had just caught his war prize.

"Running Wolf?" She stepped out of the tub-shower carefully and wrapped the towel around her body as best as she could. It was hard to find towels that covered her full figure.

"I think I'm going to add big bath towels to my list. I hate these small ones. They always open up when I move," she mumbled and finally broke away from his stare. "Did you take the other towel? I'd like to dry my hair with it. As it is, it's going to take a while for it to dry."

Kizzy slowly lifted her head. He held out his hand to her.

Tonight, was different than their wedding night. This man would demand her obedience. The Master was now front and center, just like in one of her erotic novels.

Kizzy placed her hand into his. "Good girl," was all he said, but it felt as if the sun shone down, lighting her world.

Running Wolf pulled her to him and placed a kiss on the top of her head before wrapping his arm around her and guiding her into the room. One of the chairs from the table sat in front of a full-length mirror. A towel covered the seat, but Velcro straps circled the arm rests and front legs.

She swallowed as he led her to the chair, stripping her of her towel. He laid it on the back of the leather chair. "Sit, please."

Kizzy hated to be in front of a full-length mirror naked, but she did what he asked. Kneeling, Running Wolf reached up and cupped her cheek. "Tonight, is all about trust and making our bond stronger. I know you understand some of what is going on, but let me explain. I am a Master. I expect full control in the bedroom and sometimes out of it. Is that understood?" He stuffed a pillow behind her, scooting her ass to the edge.

Her hands started to get sweaty, even after the shower. "Yes, Master."

"Very good." He stood, taking the arm closest to him and Velcroing it to the armrest. "Any time what I do makes you nervous, say yellow and we will pause and assess the situation, but if anything hurts, you will yell red. Then everything stops. Is that understood?"

"Yes, Master." The words came out easier the second time as he ran his hands down her left leg to her knee. Running Wolf reached over to the dresser behind him and grabbed a piece of rope, tucking it under her leg then around the metal part to the armrest spreading her open. "This won't be too tight. I don't want bruises on your body unless I put them there." He fastened her ankle next. "How does this feel? Too tight?"

Her mouth dry, Kizzy licked her lips. "No, Master," she squeaked.

He stood and disappeared behind her then returned with a bottle of water. "Take a drink, please."

"How did you know?" She reached for the bottle, but he shook his head, taking her free arm and putting it on the armrest.

"I will hold the bottle. And I know because I recognize the signs. To be a Master or Dom, one must pay close attention to one's subs or slaves."

She frowned while taking a drink.

"I know you are not a slave, but I believe you are very close. I've been studying your actions. Am I wrong?" He took the water bottle away and placed it on the dresser then hooked the Velcro around her arm and grabbed another piece of rope.

He spoke the truth. Even when she had been furious at him, Kizzy had sought his guidance on things. Ever since that first day after she had been hurt, Kizzy had looked toward Running Wolf. It had been natural for her. Even though Kizzy had only known him for a few days, Running Wolf had slipped past her defenses.

"How? I sit here and remember everything, and I don't know how I could do this. I've never accepted someone so quickly."

After securing her, Running Wolf cupped her face and kissed her lips before placing a hand over her heart. "Because we were born to be together. Our souls were meant for each other. I need to care for you, give you everything you need. Your pleasure, pain, food, and anything else you crave. Right now, your pussy lips are wet, your nipples are hard. Even though you don't like the mirror in front of you, you have allowed me to place you there because you trust me Kizzy. You know I would lay my life down for you. That is how much I love you."

No one since her parents had given her unconditional love. She closed her teary eyes, trying to get her emotions under control.

"No, Little Gypsy. open those beautiful eyes let me in." Running Wolf kissed each lid.

A few tears rolled down her cheek. He carefully wiped them away and, moving behind her, he took a brush from the table and started to carefully work all the knots out of her hair. His eyes never left hers in the mirror. "Now tell me how you feel?"

His beautiful wife sputtered, and Running Wolf had to hide his smile. He would break her of her habit of burying her feelings. "Now, Kizzy."

"Overwhelmed, like a part of me has been hidden that I didn't know was there. Questioning myself as to how quickly I accepted all of this." She lowered her head, and he reached over her and smacked her pussy lips with the brush.

She jumped.

"Keep your eyes on me, and I have explained the reason why this was so quick. We were born for each other. Your heart and soul were waiting for me. I'm afraid you're getting hurt. All those emotions hit you hard." He spoke close to her ear. "Never doubt yourself, Kizzy. Sure, we all make mistakes, including me, but we learn from them." He sucked on her ear lobe then bit it before standing up and starting to braid her hair. For what he had planned, her hair would need to be bound. "I'm waiting." He smacked the side of her right breast then pulled her chair back a few feet, giving him the room he'd need for his playing.

"I trust you more than any person, except my parents. Maybe even more than my brother. I'm afraid, Master."

Taking in every movement, he slid his hands down and cupped her breasts. "You are not the only one who is afraid, Little Gypsy. I'm afraid I will fail to protect you again, that I'll lose you to some crazy off the street. I'm afraid I don't have what it takes to lead our people, but fear is good. It means we are always changing, looking for ways to improve ourselves." He placed a kiss on her neck then sucked her skin, marking her, claiming what was his.

His lovely lady was about to have little hickeys all over, along with stripes from his flogger. He kissed the mark he had left, rolling her nipples between his fingers, pinching them. "Your skin marks so easily. I can't wait to see how you take to my flogger."

She sucked in her breath, and tiny goose bumps rose on her skin. Running Wolf kissed a path down her chest to her nipple, sucking it into his mouth, loving the taste of his woman.

Running Wolf put a series of marks on her breasts then all

down her stomach. Kneeling between her legs, he took a deep breath. She smelled sweet, and her pussy glistened with the desire that he had created.

He reached up and separated her pussy lips. Her little clit was swollen and needy, but it would have to wait as he licked all around it, not touching it. He slid a finger down and pushed it into her, enjoying her reactions to his touch. Kizzy's head fell back, and she moaned.

The little spot inside her was easy to find with his finger. Her whimpers only made his cock ache, and the need to carry her to the bed to take her was strong, but he would not do that yet.

He pulled his finger out and sucked the juices off it before pushing the chair back a little more. It was time to play a little. Running Wolf stood. Her skin was flushed, his Little Gypsy's eyes glazed over. He went to the spare bed and dug into the bag he carried on the back of the bike.

"Where did that come from?" Kizzy tried to focus on what he was doing.

"It's your back rest, from the bike." He pulled out the lube, the plug he had picked up for her. "Tonight, you'll wear this. I want to get you ready to take me." Running Wolf moved back between her legs, lubing his fingers.

"Running Wolf?" Her voice shook.

He kept his gaze on her as he slowly slid his finger into her ass, working the lube in deep. "Relax. Take a deep breath."

"Relax while you have your finger is in my ass? Were you smoking some of that home-grown stuff?"

Chapter Twenty-One

"To truly love someone is to trust them enough to stick things in places where they don't belong." Kizzy, Running Wolf's wife.

Kizzy was all about the Master and submitting to her man, but when his big fat finger breached a place no one had ever touched, his Little Gypsy was ready to dance on his damn head and not the one he thought with. "That was not very nice, and you're glaring at me?"

He smacked her pussy hard, his hand covering the spot he had hit. The heat from the pain of his smack, his finger now all the way inside her.... Kizzy never experienced so many conflicting feelings.

"Have a little trust in your husband." His fingers slid out of her ass and something cold and slimy pushed into her. "This little toy will start the process of opening you back here. So one day you will be able to take my cock. Maybe I'll fill your pussy with a toy and fuck your ass." He stopped talking and sucked her clit into his mouth, nipping it then lapping away the sting.

She was just about to come when her sadistic husband pushed the big ball thing all the way into her ass, denying her orgasm. "You—"

He stood and grabbed a flogger then brought it down on her right breast. "Not a word, unless you need to tell me to slow down, say yellow, remember? Or if something hurts my Little Gypsy or you have a cramp, yell out red so I know to help you." He traced the area he had hit with his fingers. "You mark so pretty." Running Wolf placed a mark on her other breast and didn't stop.

Her skin was warm, and she needed so bad. The flogger touched everywhere, all around her pussy, which seemed to ache with need.

She writhed, attempting to move.

"Easy, love." Running Wolf lifted her up and carried her to the bed. "You're so wet," he mumbled, placing kisses down her stomach. He cupped and squeezed her breasts as he moved between her legs. "I can't wait, Little Gypsy." He brought her hands above her head. "Hold on to the headboard, baby, and don't let go."

She looked up at her warrior man, his cock rubbing against her pussy lips.

"You're so wet and needy."

"Please," she begged, but didn't have to wait long as Running Wolf thrust inside her. "Too much!" Kizzy whimpered and released the headboard.

He bit her breast. "Put them back." He licked away the pain of the bite.

"How are you?"

"K, betterrrr," she said as her ass started to vibrate. "What's that?"

He did not answer her question, just moaned and started to move in and out of her. "Damn that feels good. I won't last long." Her skin tingled each time his connected with hers. "I want to touch you please."

Running Wolf nipped her chin. "Wrap your arms around me and hold on, Little Gypsy. We're going to fly."

He was right. In a matter of seconds, the vibration increased, and Running Wolf reached between them and rubbed her swollen clit. "Come!" he growled, his thrust hard and quick.

Kizzy screamed into his mouth as he covered her, kissing her, tongue dancing with hers, making love to her mouth as he did her body. Tears rolled down her checks, she trembled, and grabbed hold of his shoulders, burying her nails into his skin. Never had she felt so close to anyone. Her heart was bare as was her soul.

Running Wolf broke the kiss, staring down at her. "Oh, Little Gypsy." He gently rolled over, holding onto her as she cried, her orgasm slowly dying down as his seed filled her. "I've got you, my wife, love. Know I will always be beside you, making sure you are cared for." He rubbed her back. "Sleep, little Kizzy, sleep. Tomorrow will bring a new day and another miracle addition to our lives. Our little girl will rest in your arms soon."

She closed her eyes. "I love you," Kizzy whispered, meaning it, knowing he was her life.

Running Wolf straightened the room, being as quiet as he could, his wife still sleeping. He had awakened her in the middle of the night, possessing her again and taking out the butt plug.

Her little glares had made him hard as a rock, and Running Wolf hadn't planned on taking her again, but his little submissive needed to learn, especially on the road they were taking. Her acceptance of his word would be important.

"Hmm, I think I like the stare I was getting last night better than that frown," she mumbled, peeking up at him. "What time is it?"

"We have a little time before we have to go." Running Wolf placed his bag on the other bed before covering his wife with his body. "So you like me staring at you, do you?" He uncovered her breasts for his view and sucked her nipple into his mouth. "Too bad we don't have enough time to continue this, but tonight, honey, we will continue your training." He sat up, resting a little bit of his weight on her hips as he ran his finger around her nipple.

She sat up and ran her hands over his chest. "You're dressed." Kizzy tried to pull his tank top out of his jeans.

He captured her wrists, stopping her movements. "No, Little Gypsy, you'll have to wait until tonight. We have to get ready because I would like to be on the road today even if it's a half-day's ride." He kissed her check and jumped off the bed. "Go clean up, sweetie. I'll gather our stuff."

"Running Wolf, aren't you scared? I mean, every time we turn around something seems to be happening. Can we really keep that little girl safe?" Kizzy pulled her knees up, hugging them, appearing so unsure and lost it was breaking his heart.

He sat on the side of the bed and lifted her into his lap. "Miranda will be fine, and so will we. Is it going to be rough? Yes. But if we stick together, not just us three, but your family, mine, and the others joining us, we'll do this. Believe, Little Gypsy," he kissed her lips softly and hugged her tight. "And as to your question, yes, I'm scared. Who wouldn't be? Our world is changing, and we have to go with the signs, but I will be by your side always."

She kissed his chest. "And why do I get the feeling you'll be bossing me around most of the time?" Kizzy nipped his chest and jumped off his lap, running to the bathroom. But he caught her before she could set foot into it, lifting her up against the wall and biting her boob.

"Ouch." She glared at him, rubbing the spot.

"I bite back, Little Gypsy, and as for bossing, you know I'm a dominant man. With the way things are now, I need you to listen to me, Kizzy. I don't want to have to repeat something when it could be your life or someone else's."

"I won't. This is all new to me. I would never question your judgment, but you'll allow me to help?"

"Always, Little Gypsy," he said as someone pounded on the door. "Now, we're late." He kissed her and lowered her to the ground, slapping her ass. "I laid out some clothes for you. Hurry up."

"You laid clothes out for me?"

"Move it." He shut her in the bathroom and opened the outside door to Dark Horse. "Come in. We're running a little late. Did you get the route planned out?"

"Yes, the cop showed us a way around. When do you want to pull out? Your bike has been loaded in the trailer. You sure you don't want us to drive the Hummer? That thing is big." Dark Horse said as Kizzy came out carrying her toothbrush and hairbrush, her hair pulled back into a braid, and the outfit he'd laid out showed off her curves yet was practical for travel.

"I like your hair down," he said as she moved to his side.

"But it's a pain. I'll take it down when we stop for the night," Kizzy said, but he stood there staring at her, and she sighed and undid her hair. "We have to pick up Miranda, first at ten, and the judge wants to meet us at his safe place. We'll leave around eleven. I want us all to eat first so we don't have to stop till suppertime."

"Do you think the judge's wife will be there? I copied a few things down for her, some herbs she might consider growing to help with healing and such. Plus, I want to thank her again. The lists she has given me will help us a lot." Kizzy ran her fingers through her loose hair.

"Thank you and, yes, she'll be there." He kissed the top of her head. "Grab your coat and purse. We have our little girl to pick up. Later, you can tell me when you had time to read all those lists." He patted her butt.

"That's easy. I woke up about two. Guess I was a little nervous, and reading calms me. So I grabbed my little light and sat on the other bed so I didn't wake you."

They followed Dark Horse outside, the sun just coming up, and the warm air hit him. "I don't like the idea of you out of our bed when I'm sleeping, Little Gypsy."

"I like to read at night, and you need your sleep just as much as I do. Maybe in time I'll stop waking up, but then again, maybe it's a good thing, depending on when our little girl wakes for her feedings. Are we going to make it in time for her morning bottle?" She reached for her phone.

"Of course. That is one of the reasons I've made sure we were up. Sun Bull, did you put the mini cooler in the car? We'll have to make up bottles before we leave," he said.

"I did that last night, too. Julie gave me a diaper bag filled with washed glass bottles for us to start out with, so I made them. Crap. I left them in the fridge." She'd whirled around to go back to the room when he snaked his arm around her, throwing Dark Horse the key to the room.

"You get in the car. Dark Horse will get them." He kissed her cheek. "I have a feeling you will be taking a nap this afternoon." He tapped her nose.

"I think you're right, but you'll let me drive if you need to rest, right?" She climbed into the car.

He reached over her and grabbed the seat belt, snapping it in place. He couldn't stop staring at her, or believing she was his. "You are my sun, Little Gypsy, and we'll see." Running Wolf kissed her nose.

Dark Horse arrived with a bag and Running Wolf waved him toward the back. "Put those in the little cooler."

Shutting her door, Running Wolf faced his men. "I want to hit Kentucky tonight. We might be late, but I want our full team together. As we get closer to Texas, I have a feeling we are going to have more stumbling blocks in our way." He lifted his head toward the south. "Even though we got the two guys, I have a feeling there was another. I want everyone on alert. Sun Bull, you will take the lead. Dark Horse, ride in front of us. Meet us at the safe zone." He moved around to the driver's side and opened the door.

"I have three men going with you to the hospital," Dark Horse said. "Plus me."

"Thanks." Running Wolf got in and started the car. "Are we ready, Kizzy?"

"I'm scared half out of my mind but ready." She rubbed her hands on her red skirt.

Running Wolf kissed the back of her hand. "We're together, no

matter what. You are never alone now

Chapter Twenty-Two

"Even with the treat of death and destruction all around them, the warmth of a baby's body against yours will replace the fear with the need to protect what is so innocent." Kizzy, Running Wolf's Wife, White Buffalo MC

Kizzy checked out every inch of her daughter's face as Miranda drank her bottle. It amazed her this little miracle was theirs. Running Wolf stood across the room, talking to Dark Horse, but every once in a while he'd glance back at her and Miranda. The man never missed a thing, well, when he was awake.

"What was that smile about?" he asked, coming over and placing a kiss on top of Miranda's head before kneeling in front of her.

"I was just thinking you are always aware of everything around you, especially when it comes to me." She patted her tiny fingers. "And her, now."

"And? I know there is more."

"Okay, well, when you're awake." She giggled.

"I don't find that funny, Little Gypsy. What if something happens to you while I'm sleeping?"

Kizzy stood and lifted Miranda to her shoulder. She patted her back, burping her. "Running Wolf, you can't be in control 100 percent of the time." She moved toward the door where the nurse waited for them.

"Go ahead and pull your car around. I'll bring her down," the nurse said, handing a large diaper bag to Running Wolf. "We threw in some extra diapers and bottles for you since you are traveling. They are all biodegradable. The judge and his wife keep us stocked up here."

Kizzy squeezed the nurse's arm. "Be safe and thank you."

The nurse shifted from foot to foot. "Would you mind if I meet you up north. I heard Detective Neil is going?"

"We would love to have you join us. The judge and his wife know how to contact us. I've left my phone number with him," Running Wolf said, and Kizzy handed her a business card.

"That is my cell number. If you need it. This is my business phone, but I carry it with me all the time. It also has my email, too." Kizzy moved toward the exit.

"I didn't know you had business cards, or a separate phone for business," he said "Don't tell me you worked last night, too?"

"I did text apologies to my customers, telling them I wouldn't be able to send them anything anytime soon, if ever again," she whispered as they exited the hospital. Running Wolf pulled her into his arms.

"Your skills will help us more than you know, but I am sorry. Seems we are all learning to cope." He hugged her tight and led her to the car. "Would you mind if we hand out your business cards to those interested in joining us?" he asked, after getting Miranda settled in her car seat and saying good-bye to the nurse.

They pulled out of the hospital parking lot with Dark Horse in front of them and two men behind them. "I have no problem with it, but I think we should do this with each safe place we know of. For example, we can set Dark Horse up with an email account right now and put it on the back of one of my cards when we get closer to Texas. But he should also get a phone just for this, to have the calls go to voice mail or something. We can pick up some more cell phones when we stop, setting them up for each safe zone, just like we are doing the CB thing," she told him as he pulled up to a log cabin. "This isn't their safe zone, is it?"

"No, the entrance is under the house. You can get in two different ways, and, from what Soaring Eagle told me, each is protected." Running Wolf parked the truck and came around to open her door.

"What a gentleman you are," she teased.

"Watch it, Little Gypsy, I won't hesitate to take you out in those woods and show you I'm not a gentleman." Running Wolf pulled her into his arms and kissed her hard, punishing her. He touched the scarf she wore around her neck. "You are stunning."

"I used to have many scarves that were my mom's, but they

were lost to me when I lost my bag. Scarves are easy to carry. When it's hot, I wrap it around my hair or twine it in a braid. I use them to dance, all sorts of things." She pulled him down, so she could speak in his ear. "You should see my midnight dance I made up. I haven't shown it to anyone. Well, it's kind of hot." She teased and moved away from him, but not before running her hand over his cock.

"Running Wolf, I'm so glad you came. Julie has been waiting for your wife," the judge said, coming up to her husband as Kizzy unhooked the carrier from the car seat.

"Move out of the way, I'll carry her, and you are so getting spanked later." He bit her neck as he lifted her out of the way then grabbed the carrier.

"Oh, my notes!" Kizzy moved to the back of the car and opened the hatch, digging in her bag. "Where...? Here we go." She grabbed the notes and swung around to Julie. "I made these out for you. I make homemade soap, shampoo, perfume, spices, and stuff like that. I've always kept a written copy of how I do it, so I figured this might help you guys. Also, there are some of those herbs on the list that help with common ailments." She closed the hatch and moved with Julie toward the house. "Do you have a camera set up to keep up with what is going on above when you're underground?"

"How would they run it when the electricity goes out?" Running Wolf and the judge joined them.

"Solar. You'd have to hide the panels, but I'd start getting as many as you can. I did research on them for my tiny house. They work great. Run your wires through the ground, keep your generator below, and extra panels also in case something happens," Kizzy told them as they stepped into the log cabin home. Running Wolf he was staring at her and so was the judge. "What?"

"You actually know about this stuff?" the judge asked.

"Excuse my husband. He sometimes forgets we have brains, too." Julie rolled her eyes. "Come on, I want to show you where I've started to set up our nursery, and I'll make sure to order those panels, we can spread them around the cabin if we have to." Julie opened up a room, and Kizzy stood there staring at the open floor. "We go down on a ladder here, but the rest of the way we'll walk." Julie went down first followed by Kizzy.

"Here, hand me the baby?" Kizzy said, but already Running Wolf was coming down the ladder with the baby. "You know I could have taken her."

"Yes, you could have, but I like carrying our daughter." Running

Wolf reached the bottom and once more slid his arm around her as the judge and Julie led the way.

"Wait, this is a mine tunnel isn't it?" Kizzy asked.

The judge turned his gaze on her. "Yes, but all operations had stopped when they were about to go down farther, which is a blessing. We have a natural pond down here, and a few animals have found their way here also. I've also had all the history to this place destroyed as far as I know. The less people remember that there was a mine, the better when the time comes."

Kizzy touched the wall on her left. "You've firmed it up with a little cement, sort of like they did in the old days when making bricks. Impressive."

Running Wolf squeezed her hand. "You impress me each time you say something, Little Witch." He kissed her knuckles as they moved around a corner and stopped, staring down at an open cavern from a rough-hewn balcony.

"Wow." Kizzy said.

Even Running Wolf was impressed at what they had seen. Little hut-like structures, at least ten of them, were built around a massive pond. Other tunnels led off into the darkness.

"Where is that light coming from?" Kizzy asked.

"We got lucky," Julie said as they moved down the sloped path. "The judge here believes the sun is being reflected from some of the gemstones in the ceiling. I don't care what it is as long as I have some natural light down here."

Running Wolf had to agree with the judge as to gemstones being the cause of the light. As they moved farther down, he noticed a few people moving around carrying boxes, building things.

"I hope to have twenty huts up for people who arrive. I have the main cabin through that tunnel there." He pointed. "I've also had eight composting toilets down that smaller tunnel away from the living quarters. Julie has started stocking up on dry shampoo, and, if she follows your directions, we can now have our own soap, too. But we do have a few people here who make soap, candles, and such, too."

"How far down are we?" Kizzy moved toward rows of potted fruit trees and plants. The nursery.

"We're about a mile down," the judge said as Miranda started to fuss.

"I bet she's wet after…" Kizzy wrinkled her nose. "Stinky little girl, that is what you are my little Miranda. Running Wolf, we didn't bring the diaper bag?"

"Not to worry." Julie ran to one of huts and came out with a little bag. "I've been putting together kits for people who might show up with children. You should find everything you need in there." Julie handed her the bag as Kizzy took off her scarf and laid it on the ground, but he took off his shirt and handed it to her.

"Use this. It's thicker." Running Wolf unhooked their beautiful little girl. "Yep, you are a little stinky," he said, laying her on his shirt and starting to unsnap her onesie."

Kizzy gaped. "You're going to change her?"

"Yes. What if you are busy and there is no one around? I will be helping with all our children," he said, almost regretting it when he opened up the diaper, activating his gag reflex.

Kizzy whistled. "She has to take after you because I could never be that stinky." She teased him as he took one of the wipes from her proceeding to clean his daughter off. But just as he grabbed the next diaper, his beautiful daughter decided she needed to pee, getting him and his shirt.

Kizzy fell on her butt next to him, laughing. The judge and his wife joined her.

Dark Horse happened to pick that time to meet them below. "Seems like your daughter just christened you."

"Keep it up," he grumbled and rolled his shirt up, keeping Miranda's little butt in the air as he quickly wiped her down again and put the fresh diaper on.. "There we go." He placed his daughter in the car seat and hooked her back up.

Kizzy wrapped the dirty diaper and wipes up together and stuffed them in the zip-up baggie in the bag. "We'll have to get you another shirt, but we'll wrap this one, and I'll wash it with the load I have already next time we stop," his wife said, stuffing his shirt in the bag.

For the next hour, Julie and Kizzy talked about what she could do with her nursery and what to plant, and all the while their daughter slept now that she had been cleaned up. As they said their good-byes to Julie and the judge, Kizzy stared up at the hill and shivered.

"Are you cold?" he asked, coming up behind her and rubbing his hands up her arms.

"No, but I have a feeling…." She stopped, facing the judge and

Julie as they got into their vehicle, heading toward town. "We need to get going."

"Kizzy, is there something we should know?"

"That's just it. I don't know what it is," she growled and got into the car. "Let's get going."

Running Wolf buckled Kizzy up. He cupped her face and kissed her lips softly. "I'm sure whatever it is, you'll figure it out."

That was when she noticed the CB radio Dark Horse must have installed in the car while they were touring. He was an amazing man, and she would make sure he and his woman would be safe before they left.

Chapter Twenty-Three

"A family can consist of anyone, blood or not. The thought of anyone in harm's way always leaves a dark spot on one's soul, but a single light can break through the darkness and give one hope."
Dark Horse, Enforcer, White Buffalo MC

The stars were bright, and her stomach rumbled. Running Wolf snorted next to her. In the back, their daughter was sound asleep after another feeding and a change of her diaper. They were now in Kentucky, heading to the city of Louisville.

Already, five new men had joined their procession of bikes and cars. "We'll be there in about ten minutes." Her husband took her hand, squeezing it. It seemed Running Wolf couldn't stop touching her, kissing her, and Kizzy wasn't going to complain.

"I'll be fine, but you should have let me drive a little," Kizzy said. "I haven't gotten to drive the car yet. Is there a reason you don't want me to drive? Did my brother talk to you?" She tried to give him the eye, but he just snorted and patted her leg.

"No, but do I need to talk to him?" he asked.

"Well, when I was in high school, I did have a few accidents, but they weren't all my fault, of course." She giggled. "That one I can actually blame on the groundhog."

"Okay spill it. What did you do to a groundhog?"

"I didn't do anything. I stopped to let the poor thing cross the road, but that fool behind me didn't appreciate it," she said. "Not only did he swerve around me and hit the animal, but the next person behind him did hit my car, sending it in the ditch." Kizzy rested her head against the window.

"You should have seen my dad and brother. Both of them just

shook their heads and had my car towed home. But I made them bury the poor groundhog before I left."

"Only you, baby, only you." He pulled into a Marriott hotel driveway.

"What are we doing here?" she asked as he stopped in front of the front doors.

He turned the car off and faced her. "I've decided since we don't have much time left before most of this is gone, we will enjoy a nice place to sleep while we travel. Plus, we need a place with a kitchen for the baby," he told her.

"You know there are cheaper places, right? Shouldn't we be saving money, since we have to buy all sorts of things for the safe zone when we get to Canada?"

"We have enough money, Kizzy. We've been saving all the money from the casino, knowing we'd need it for something. Which reminds me. Dark Horse is going to need to set up a bank account, so we'll be able to wire him money for his safe zone." Running Wolf helped her out of the car. Never had she seen so many bikes. There had to be close to five hundred.

"Well, shit. When you warriors come together, you don't do it half ass," she muttered, as a man she hadn't met came up to them. Kizzy stepped closer to Running Wolf. The man was exactly what she would have thought a biker would appear like. Pierced ear, a scar on his cheek, a beard—totally not what she would expect for a Native American.

"Night Wind, quit scaring my wife" Running Wolf wrapped his arms around her.

The man snorted but nodded to her. "You were always the lucky bastard when it came to women." His deep voice sent a shiver down her spine.

Running Wolf slapped her butt. "Only I should be sending shivers up your spine." He nipped her neck, staring down at her nipples that were now hard as rocks. "Night Wind, this is my wife, Kizzy, and our daughter Miranda." He took the carrier out of the back seat.

The large man bent down, peeking at Miranda. "Damn, she's going to be a gorgeous one, too." He winked at Kizzy. "Yep, you are a lucky bastard. It's great to meet you, Ms. Kizzy. We've heard you have done wonders for our man, and I can see it is true. There is hope once more in his eyes."

Kizzy tilted her head to side and grinned. "Your woman is

coming soon."

"What did I do to you? Is she serious?" Night Wind asked.

"I'm afraid so." Running Wolf wrapped his arm around her and guided her into the hotel, followed by Dark Horse and Night Wind. Inside, her brother and uncles waited for them, along with Soaring Eagle.

"About time you two get here with my great niece," Stephen said.

Her uncles crowded around Running Wolf and the baby. Kizzy couldn't help but laugh at the big goons going goo-goo over a tiny little female.

She moved toward the counter, planning on registering them, but Dark Horse stepped up next to her. "Where are you going, Kizzy?"

"Right here, to get us a room then food." She patted his arm. "Are you going to stay here, too? I told Running Wolf we could stay somewhere else, but I guess he wants me to be comfortable." She leaned over close to him. "Little does he know I grew up sleeping outside more than I did inside."

Kizzy moved up to the lady who greeted her. "We need a room with a fridge, please." She pulled out her wallet. This time, Kizzy was going to pay for something.

"We'll need a room next to them also, please, and you can put it on here," the big jerk, Dark Horse, said, pushing her aside.

"Hey, I was going to pay for that."

"No, you know better." Running Wolf arrived at her side and tugged on her hair.

"Fine."

"I have to say, my niece is a beauty. I'm going to have to teach my boys to keep an eye on her. So where do you want to eat?" Mason asked, holding Miranda.

She scanned the big area and noticed a restaurant to the left. "Why don't we eat here? We can get settled in and come on down to eat. That way we don't have to unhitch the car from the trailer." Her stomach tightened and palms got sweaty. "Shit." She moved away from Running Wolf, slowly scanning the room, but Dark Horse, Sun Bull, and Running Wolf surrounded here.

"How am I supposed to see what I need to?" Kizzy froze then flung herself at Dark Horse, kicking the back of his legs and sending him to the floor as a gun went off.

Shouts, cries filled the air as Running Wolf's people ran after the man who took off out the door. "Are you okay, Dark Horse?" she asked, moving off of him. She flinched, her thigh hurting.

"Well crap."

A red stain appeared on her skirt.

Running Wolf knelt down next to her and lifted her skirt, exposing her leg. He said nothing to her, but Kizzy could feel the anger radiating from him.

"I wasn't going to let him get shot," Kizzy said, knowing it wasn't bad, a scratch.

Running Wolf cupped her chin and lifted her head so she was staring up at him. "They are here to help protect you."

"I helped them protect themselves," she said not giving an inch. "Didn't I tell you earlier I wasn't useless?"

Her uncle Stephan came up. "Management wants us to move on."

"Really?" Running Wolf moved to the counter as the police showed up.

"Help me up," she asked her uncle, holding out her hand. He ignored it and made room for Red Hawk.

"I swear you are going to be my best patient you keep this up. Let me see your leg." Red Hawk knelt down next to her.

"It's just a scratch." She lifted her skirt. "I hope they caught the asshole. He ruined my skirt, and I saved for this one."

Red Hawk pushed on the area around the wound. "Dark Horse, grab my bag. She'll do fine if I just wrap it. You're a bleeder. That is why there is so much blood," he said as he took the bag from Dark Horse.

"You okay, Dark Horse?" she asked.

He turned and headed for Running Wolf.

Now what the hell did I do?

***

Running Wolf waited for Kizzy to get off the phone with room service. She hadn't said a word to any of them after thanking Red Hawk for bandaging her up, but, then again, Running Wolf hadn't encouraged any talking either. He was still furious the other member of the Irons had gotten that close to her.

Right now, Dark Horse was getting the information they wanted from the man, before they handed him over to the police.

"Dinner will be here in thirty minutes." She got off the bed and went to move around him, but he gently pulled her into his arms, holding her. At first, his Little Gypsy was stiff in his arms, but soon she relaxed, resting her head on his chest and...crying. Her tears wet his shirt.

Sitting on the bed, Running Wolf lifted Kizzy up, placing her on his lap. "Why the tears? Are you hurting?"

She shook her head. "You won't let me help, and you get mad when I try to. Dark Horse won't talk to me. I feel useless, like a little kid." Her tear-filled eyes lifted to stare at him. "Marriage is supposed to be about sharing, and right now...." She stopped. "Was what I did so wrong?" She shook her head. "Doesn't matter if it was." Kizzy wiped the big tears dripping down her cheeks. "Because I'd do it again in a heartbeat. I'm sorry if I disappointed you, but Dark Horse's life is more important than you being upset." She lifted her chin, waiting.

"My silly Little Gypsy. I wasn't upset about that, well, maybe a little. The thought of you getting hurt again drives me crazy. But I was more furious at myself for not finding that ass back where we were. All of this could have been prevented if—" She placed her finger on his lips.

"We learn from our mistakes. I'm glad we're staying in the room tonight. I'm mentally and physically drained." She placed a soft kiss on his chin. "I love you, Running Wolf." She slipped off his lap. "I'm going to take a hot bath. I'll rewrap the wound when I get out. I have gauze in my bag. I need a nice hot bubble bath. Baby has been fed, burped, and changed. You go do what you are dying to do."

Running Wolf listened to Kizzy trying to sing to the soft song playing on her phone. She might be a great dancer, but his wife couldn't carry a note at all. He pulled out his cell phone and called Dark Horse.

"We'll be there in two minutes. We had to wait for the jacket to arrive, and Penn sewed on my patch for her," he said.

"Good. She's getting in the tub, so right now would be perfect," Running Wolf said.

Dark Horse laughed. "Only you would have us present her coat to her while she's soaking."

"Kizzy believes she's not helping, that she does nothing, so this will come at a perfect time." Running Wolf rose, shutting his phone off as he heard his men move in the hall. Soaring Eagle, Dark Horse, Penn, Night Wind, Sun Bull, would all be out there.

Epilogue

"Only time will tell how many of us survive the dark days, but our love for each other and the respect we share for what is around us will never stop, no matter how bad it gets." He had a feeling it was going to get much worse." Running Wolf, President, White Buffalo MC

Kizzy had just closed her eyes when Running Wolf came into the bathroom, stripping out of his jeans. "Scoot up, Little Gypsy. I want to hold my wife." He stepped into the tub behind her.

The bubbles covered her, her favorite lavender bubble bath she made herself. Kizzy had also put a moisturizer in the soap to make her skin super soft.

"Damn, this stuff is awesome. Let me guess. You made it?" He pulled her back up against his chest.

"Yep, and I have twenty bottles in my house. I'll have to make more, so we'll have it stocked up. I like this, you holding me, the music playing...." It was playing until Sun Bull turned it off and barged into the bathroom followed by Dark Horse, Night Wind, and Soaring Eagle.

"Okay, this is really not a good time guys." She slid farther down into the water.

"Actually, it's a perfect time," Running Wolf said, holding her still.

Soaring Eagle stepped forward and knelt before the tub. "You have honored us. Not only have you joined your life force with Running Wolf, you have proven that you are for the whole. Dark Horse is like a son to me as these men here in this room are. In saving Dark Horse's life, you are now the daughter of my blood."

Soaring Eagle reached for the knife he kept at his waist and sliced his finger while Running Wolf lifted her hand, offering it to Soaring Eagle.

She looked back at him, and he nodded. Oh, she knew what was going to happen, but Kizzy didn't believe it was still done.

He took her finger in his old hand and cut it, holding it as he placed his bloody one to hers, wrapping it with a leather piece Sun Bull handed him. "Please allow me, Soaring Eagle, to call this brave girl daughter, to love and protect as my own," he said.

A light breeze she thought touched her cheek, and then Kizzy smelled him, her father. Tears filled her eyes as his spirit filled the room. The lights flickered and a pressure could be felt on her finger.

"It is done. You are my daughter now, and I'm going to go peek at my granddaughter," Soaring Eagle said, unwrapping their fingers and leaning over to kiss the cheek her father had touched. "I'm proud to have a daughter with such strength and courage."

Kizzy's eyes filled with tears as she slid her hand back into the water. Dark Horse took Soaring Eagle's spot. "I want to apologize, little sister, for not speaking to you earlier, but words could not be formed. No one but my brothers and Soaring Eagle have ever cared as much as you have." He leaned over and kissed her lips softly, earning a growl from Running Wolf.

"Hurry up," he said, pushing his friend back.

"This was sent to us a couple of days ago, but I have personally added your first patch." Dark Horse accepted a leather coat from Night Wind. "A woman from one of our local tribes makes them. Don't ask me how she knows our sizes or when we earn it, but she does. Her timing is always perfect, too." Dark Horse stood and let the long duster unfold.

The coat was dark red, embroidered with beads of all colors. It was the most beautiful thing she had ever seen. But when he turned the coat around, the tears she had been holding back rolled down her cheeks. A small rose heart patch was on the back, with the words *My sister of the heart, I thank you. May the sun always shine upon you and the wind be at your back.*

"What is that?" Kizzy pointed to the dark spot under the words.

"Dark Horse's blood. You bled for him. He honors you with his blood. It's also his way of showing everyone if they hurt or touch you, they'll have to answer to him personally. But if you look below his patch, Night Wind has added the beads of our tribe or group. To receive those beads, you must have every member of our group agree on it. They value your life as part of the whole. You see, Little Gypsy, you have done something. You give us hope to go on. Right now, you are the heart of our tribe. As every woman who joins one of my brothers, your heart will only grow stronger. It won't die out, but live. You are the beginning of our journey," Running Wolf told her as the men left them alone.

Running Wolf lifted her so she was facing him, placing her on top of him, careful of her leg. He cupped her cheeks and kissed each eye. "Never let us hear you say you do nothing. I love you, my Little Gypsy and I need you by my side for however long we have. You and that little girl out there are the beginning of our journey."

Kizzy said nothing. She couldn't if she'd wanted to, so she leaned forward, hugging him tight, hoping he understood how much this meant to her.

"You have a new name. Soaring Eagle has agreed if you don't want to be called it, you don't have to, but you are now called, Dancing Hearts. With your new name, our life begins anew."

Coming Soon!

The Heart's Dark Hunger

Book 2

Dark Horse's Book: Texas

"Dark shadows can always be pushed away by the sun, but when the sun itself is damaged, only time will heal the wounds," *Dark Horse, Enforcer, White Buffalo MC*

The wind blew against his skin. He wore no helmet. If he was going to die, then so be it. Dark Horse peeked in his rearview mirror and snorted. Dancing Hearts was bobbing in her seat in the car behind him. His sister of the heart was most likely singing, too, and he was so glad he wasn't in the vehicle with Running Wolf.

Would his woman sing off key? He had dreamed of her last night. She was stunning, with long blonde hair and big green eyes, but the sadness in them haunted him now.

The knife scars on her cheek and neck were not the only scars on his woman's body, but, like him, she had survived. But those who have hurt her would know no mercy. Where Running Wolf had been gentle with those who hurt Dancing Hearts, his enemy would know this warrior believed in old-time punishments.

Fire ants, staking a man in the middle of a fire would be just the beginning. To hear his yelling, pleas would be music to his dark soul, but could Lark hold on until they got there? Lark. Just saying her name made her sound so real.

"Only one more day, my Dark Rose," he said to the wind, ready to destroy any Irons that stepped in his way.

About the Author

Trinity Blacio is the #1 Amazon-romance bestselling author of such paranormal erotic romance series as the *Running in Fear* and *Masters of the Cats* series, as well as a number of dark fantasy, erotic romance, erotic horror and ménage titles. She is a PAN member of the Ohio chapter of Romance Writers of America and is the bestselling author of a paranormal stepbrothers series that made her an All Romance eBooks and Siren bestselling author.

Coming from a split family, Trinity Blacio has lived in Minnesota, California, Michigan, Florida, but eventually settled in the state where she was born—Ohio. She has an Associates Degrees in Psychology and Social Work from Lorain County Community College and a Bachelor's Degree in Psychology from Cleveland State University.

You will find her on Facebook, Twitter and Goodreads. She loves to talk with all her fans

www.ingramcontent.com/pod-product-compliance
Lightning Source LLC
Chambersburg PA
CBHW061247170626
46809CB00007B/2887